JG NOLAN was born and rais  a sleepy village in Shropshire and writing stories and playing football as a child.

He has been a teacher for many years, working mainly with children who have had difficult beginnings in life. He strongly believes in positive thinking and feels most things are achievable if you put your mind to it.

When his football-mad son Robbie was much younger, he kept breaking bones and was told by the doctors that he would never play football again. It was during one of JG Nolan's many lengthy stays visiting his son in the local children's hospital that the idea for his first book, Jump!, drifted into his mind.

Following on from the success of Jump! JG Nolan was keen to explore the story of Robbie Blair's footballing friend Jamie, and this led him to delve into another journey of adversity, determination and recovery.

The first two books in the Jump! series reflect JG Nolan's deep-rooted interest in sporting prowess, mental strength and history.

When he's not busy battering away at his old computer, conjuring up new tales, JG Nolan can either be found playing squash or strumming his guitar. For many years he tried to "make it" in his indie rock band, The Poet Dogs.

He still writes songs now. When he has the time.

Connect with JG Nolan on TikTok and Instagram @JGNolan3

CARINA ROBERTS is an award-winning artist and illustrator who loves creating characters and telling stories. Carina spent her childhood drawing, reading and befriending animals - it was in these first few years that her dream to be an illustrator was born.

Carina grew up near Bristol. As a shy student in her early years, she was drawn to subjects that allowed her thoughts to bubble and overflow (as well as any sports that allowed her to run as fast as she could!). She particularly enjoyed discovering stories that focused on feelings—her curiosity and creativity were always encouraged by her family. She also discovered that drawing helped her to feel calm, even before presentations or exams.

When Carina was approached in 2021 by JG Nolan and Siân Bağcı about Jump! she was immediately drawn to the character of Robbie, and the elements of Celtic history and Scottish landscape woven throughout the story. For the second book in the series, she was excited to immerse herself in Jamie's world and take every step of her journey with her.

Carina specialises in creating books, particularly for young readers. She loves to be outside in all weathers, sketchbook and snacks in her backpack, capturing the wildness of her home in Wales – where the skies are always perfectly, beautifully imperfect.

Website: https://carinarobertsillustration.co.uk
Instagram: https://www.instagram.com/carinarobertsillustration/
X/Twitter: https://twitter.com/RobertstheRed

JUMP2
"You are enough!"

Written by
JG Nolan

Illustrated by
Carina Roberts

Produced by
Siân Bağcı

Published in 2024 by Sergar Creative Limited
Copyright © JG Nolan
Illustrations © Carina Roberts

The author and publisher gratefully thank Tom Bukovac for providing permission for content included in Chapter 14.

All photos included in montages are from private family collections.

ISBN 9781739208424 (paperback) ISBN 9781739208431 (ebook)
British Library Cataloguing in Publication Data
A CIP catalogue record for this book is available from the British Library.

Cover design, page design and typesetting by sian@sergarcreative.co.uk
For further information, please visit www.linktr.ee/sergarcreative

For Rosanne, Alex and Robbie x

In the middle of winter, I at last discovered there
was within me an invincible summer!
Albert Camus

This summer I went swimming
This summer I might have drowned
But I held my breath and I kicked my feet
And I moved my arms around
I moved my arms around

Loudon Wainwright III The Swimming Song

Acknowledgements

JUMP2 could not have happened without the support and encouragement of family, friends and strangers.

Thanks again to my dad, Cyril, for always believing in me.

Thanks again to Siân Bağcı of Sergar Creative for doing such an excellent job of producing the whole project and trying so hard to keep me on the straight and narrow! A problematic, unenviable task!

Massive thanks to Rosanne for once again using her many years of experience as a teacher and a reader to provide lots of valuable feedback.

Big thanks to my son Alex Nolan for getting stuff done. Top man.

Talking of feedback, thanks so much to our merry band of Alpha readers who kindly read the first draft of Jump2 and provided some really helpful and constructive comments – so cheers to Ted Eames, Lee Picken, Charles Hart, Julie Evenson, Hilary Jones, Savannah Millan-Gibson and Rosanne.

Brilliant to have Ted Eames on board as developmental editor for Jump2. You have the perfect blend of being a bit "out there" but also rigorous and wise.

I am grateful to Yasmin Yarwood of Meticulous Proofreading for such an enlightening experience and for sorting my hyphens from my en dashes!

Many thanks to Kacper Pagorek for his unflustered attitude when helping us with our website and all things techy!

Cheers, Ben Schur, for your insightful conversations regarding sport, psychology, life and the universe.

Thank you, Ross Frisby, for similarly always being at hand to provide little nuggets of wisdom about the workings of the sporting mind.

Thank you to Lee Picken from Shrewsbury Squash and Racketball Club for always being around for me and always available for a chat. I seem to do lots of chatting!

Talking of the squash club – my second home – thank you to Chris Wase for his helpful advice, support and positivity throughout the whole project.

Thanks also to Duncan Moselhi, Shropshire squash legend, for allowing me to dress him up in medieval outfits and challenge him to bizarre squash match-ups for TikTok.

Thanks to Dan Elliot, an elite Ironman and triathlete, for providing valuable insights into how an elite athlete thinks, behaves and competes.

Similarly, thank you, Aaron Williams, for always showing interest in my books and advising me on football skills and fitness.

Alex Williams, thanks for your continued interest and positivity regarding my creative projects.

Finally, thanks to Tom Bukovac for inspiring my writing over the years with his wonderful tunes and musings on life - The Great Bukovski.

So, thank you ALL for playing your part. Like Jamie, I can find life difficult sometimes, but have learnt, over the years that sport, humour, positivity and human contact have always been invaluable in pulling me out of a low spot and keeping me in a good place.

Thank you, one and all.

Until next time,

JG Nolan

Dear Diary

Am I actually still alive? Would you tell me if I wasn't?

I guess I am writing this, so I must be. Sort of. But you wouldn't say anything anyway, would you?

It's all one-way traffic with you. I tell you everything, but what do I get in return?

Nothing. Well, I have had better days, I must confess. I'd been so looking forward to the game. A quarter-final. What could be better? Well, a semi-final and a final, I suppose. But it's what we'd been working for.

Isn't it?

But it came back. This time worse than before. Much worse.

We were home. Expected to win. We play Paisley in the league and are normally too good for them. They're a big physical side but a bit slow. That's what Robbie says. He always says that though!

I felt ok in the warm-up. Normal. Standard. First half was tight, nothing special, but then out of nothing they scored. A scrappy finish. A goalie error. Second half. Then it happened. I was one on one with the keeper. I've practised this a thousand times with Robbie. He was by my side. Always. Robbie was always there. I felt no different to normal.

"Jamie, shoot!" came the cry. The same familiar voice. The same warm smile. "Shoot, Jamie!"

I turned to the sideline. To the voice. To my mum. Mum.

And that's the last thing I remember.

We lost by the way. That's what they told me. In the hospital.

Anyway. I'm done. I don't really feel like writing much. I don't really feel like thinking or doing anything. I hate being like this.

My dad brought me my diary. He thought it would help me. I guess he's right. Maybe. Night.

Chapter 1
Jamie

Jim looked at the girls who were standing in front of him in two loose rows.

He was a wiry man with sharp, angular features and stubble. The girls liked Jim. He laughed with them, but they knew when he was annoyed and when to listen. He'd taught most of the team for years since they were "wee bairns," as he said.

The newest girl on the team was Jamie. She joined halfway through last season, and this was her first full season. She was four-teen years old, a slim girl with long curly hair that she normally scraped back into a ponytail—like most footballers—that is, most girl footballers.

Jamie had always wanted to play football, as far as she could remember. Her mum said she had no interest in dolls as a little girl and was at her happiest in the back garden kicking and chasing a ball under the blue skies of her childhood. And dreaming, dreaming of playing football as the birds sang.

Back where they used to live, Jamie had done the usual after-school clubs and football training. She'd joined an U10s and an U11s boys' team. There were no girls' teams. Jamie didn't mind and was quicker and more skilful than most of the boys she played against. She nor-mally played on the wing. She could use her pace there. Cutting in from the right. She had a lethal right foot. Everyone said it.

But then everything changed. The blue skies became grey, and Jamie thought she would never hear the birds sing again.

Chapter 2
The Move

When they first moved to Clydebank, Jamie was very shy. It was all new and different. Not what she was used to. And, of course, it was different now because now it was just her and Dad.

Mum was gone.

After it happened, Jamie didn't talk to anyone for about a year. Or at least that's what it seemed like to her dad. The smiles and laughter vanished, and Jamie retreated to the shadows. She stayed in her bedroom instead of playing football. She looked at her garden through her bedroom window. It was the same garden, but it now seemed different. A mile away. The whole house felt different now. Her dad lost himself in his university work. And Jamie lost herself in her thoughts.

Then, one day, it happened.

Out of the blue, her dad announced that they were moving.

"I've got a job in Glasgow, at the university," he told her, during a typically rushed breakfast.

"Glasgow?" Jamie replied. "That's miles away. How you gonna do that?"

"We'll be moving."

"Moving?"

"Aye, Jamie. But I think it will be good for us."

Jamie felt her heart racing. Her breathing quickly became shallow. Her eyes welled up.

"But we cannae leave the house! We cannae leave Mum!"

Her dad stood up and went over to Jamie. He put his arm around her and held her tight. He was crying too, but she couldn't see that.

"I know, love. I know, love. But maybe it will be good for us. And she'll still be with us, Jamie. In our hearts."

And that was that. About one month later, they were all packed. The removal van had all their belongings. Jamie had said goodbye to all her friends at school and been given a lovely card that they'd all made. Jamie hugged them all and promised to keep in touch.

Now it was her home she had to say goodbye to. The home she had known all her eleven and a half years. The walls were bare now. All the family photos and pictures of Mum had been taken down. It seemed different now. Empty. Jamie's breathing quickened again and her eyes twitched. She gulped. She was going to walk around the house, her home, one more time. With her mum. But she couldn't. She couldn't bear it. So she ran to the van. And didn't look back.

She couldn't look back. For now.

Dear Diary

Yesterday was horrendous. Literally the worst yet.

I woke up feeling fine. That's the thing. How can things change so quickly? I've never been able to get my head around that. One minute, the sun's shining, the sky is blue, and you're running to the ice cream van. The next moment, someone's run over your pet cat. He's lying there motionless on the road. I've always struggled with that.

How can you be running around full of life, vibrant, alive, but the next moment something happens and that's all snuffed out in an instant?

We've been doing Shakespeare at school. Maybe that's what Macbeth was on about. "Out, out, brief candle." Anyway, I played football today. It was a big deal because it was a semi-final. Robbie was there. My dad was there.

We lost. And I will never play again.

Night.

Dear Diary

The girls were full of it at school.

I'd only known Jim for a while, but he seemed a good guy. Apparently, one of the parents made an annoying comment on the team WhatsApp group and it had literally kicked off. He reckoned they should be training more blah blah blah. Anyway, the girls reckon, even though they've never met him before, that this dad was pretty annoying. Sounds about right because we've never actually seen him at a game. Well, anyway, Jim's gone now. Just like that. Power of the internet.

Anyway, I digress. That's a cool word, isn't it? It means to leave the main subject temporarily in speaking or in writing. I think it sounds like a type of perfume. 'Digress, by some posh French perfumery.' For the record, I think I digress a lot.

What do you think?

Chapter 3
The Coach

He stood there looking at them.

Stout with a bald head. Rugged, broad shoulders. Full kit, coaching top with initials. And shin pads. Shin pads!

"So!" he said.

So! So!

So, who starts anything off with so? Don't trust them.

"So!" he went on. "I've seen ye last games. Ye nae fit enough. That's my big thing. Nae by a long stretch."

He pointed at Paisley. "Ye's quick." He pointed at Isla. "Ye's skilful." He pointed at Lorna. "Ye can tackle." He then pointed at all of them. "But none of ye, NONE OF YE, ARE FIT! NONE OF YE ARE FIT!"

Bruce then pointed at Jamie aggressively.

"You need to take a long, hard look at yourself in the mirror, Jamie. A long, hard look!"

Jamie melted into the darkness.

So, they were asked to run around the pitch. Round and round the wet, sodden pitch. When would it ever end? Eventually, they settled in the penalty area and Mark, his assistant, got the girls shooting penalties. Jamie was going through the motions, there, but not there, looking but not watching.

Later, to finish off, Bruce set up a game of 'attack and defence'. Jamie listened silently to the instructions and then looked on as the play unfolded around her. Sensing a need to do something, anything, she went in for a tackle. She slid in, missed the player and went into the sideline. She was like a puppet, crumpled and dishevelled in the driving rain. Mark helped her up and looked into her eyes.

"I think you've had enough now, lass."

Chapter 4
The School

Jamie couldn't sleep. Again.

She was back in her primary school classroom. Back in her chair. Back in her seat.

In the future, Jamie would dream about this all the time. She's thirty-three, in a flat, on her own. Her dreams of having children of her own, of having a family of her own, have vanished. She has no one and is no one. You might go searching for her football boots and her football kit and gather them up for her, ready for her next game, because she will be playing somewhere. Surely. But no, you'd be wasting your time. Because Jamie isn't a footballer any more.

The chair was small, obviously, but neat in a way, and it made her feel 'at home', like she was enclosed, but not in a bad way. Like she was in the here and now and not going down any rabbit hole any time soon.

Jamie stood up. There was a smell. Primary schools have a smell about them. Maybe all those grazed knees, unwashed hands and constant "whys" have a way of coming together and giving you that primary school smell.

She walked to the display board in front of her and saw that it was an English board. It was a nice display board, just cheap MDF as a base and colourful paper laid on top. Then laminated letters and a heading to add a little gravitas. But the real magic was when the children's work was stapled to the wall. Each crazy ascending cursive letter, each uninvited capital letter, each full stop that had jumped in like it was working for the SAS. Sweeping in, unannounced.

She looked at the writing. It was neat but vaguely untidy. It was trying to be tidy but it yearned, secretly, to be wild.

Well, don't listen to me. I don't even exist. Listen to real things. Like yourself.

Dear Diary

I hate waking up. Well, now I do anyway. When I'm asleep, I can forget it all. I'm not sad any more. And I didn't kill my mum.

It's not much to ask for, is it? OMG, that sounds so bad. I know I didn't really kill her. It's not like I pushed her off a cliff. No. But come to mention it, I do worry that I could push someone off a cliff.

We went with the school on some outward bound trip to some cliffs near Dunnet Head. I wasn't as bad as I am now. But it was still there. Growing, I guess. Maybe it's always been there.

Maybe it always will be.

Anyway, later on, we are doing some birdwatching. And it's all good. We make our way across a rickety boardwalk and up these endless wooden steps, up to this grassy verge. We then walk towards the sea. At this point, I'm just looking to where the sea meets the sky. And it's a beautiful clear blue sky which stretches out in front of us, like forever.

But then, all of a sudden, it dawns on me that I'm approaching the edge of the cliff. And then I'm there. And it's a sheer drop. I instantly feel dizzy, sick. I look down the massive drop and see the waves crashing over the rocks at the bottom. And I just think, what if I just threw myself off? Right now. Not because I'm particularly sad. Just because I can.

I instantly thought that as long as it was possible, then I would just do it. And that was it.

The trip was ruined because all I could think of was that if I was near that horrible cliff, then I would just throw myself off. Just because it was possible. So, I did everything I could to avoid cliffs, or any drops. Simple. I wouldn't go near cliffs. Or anything high. Ever. Then I would be ok. Done. Take that, Dunnet!

But it wasn't that simple. Nothing ever is. Because it was like a game of whack-a-mole: when one mole gets hit and vanishes, another rears its head. Not a cliff this time. Different every time. But always scary and always making me doubt who I am and what I'd done.

One time, me and my dad went away for a few days in the summer holidays. It was somewhere with a loch. I begged him that it wouldn't be anywhere with cliffs, which he thought was a bit weird.

I've always loved water, crystalline water. Clear and still, like I wanted my mind to be. Well, anyway, we were on our way back but still miles from anywhere. I felt a thud. Dad heard it too 'cos it was a proper thud. We turned around, which was quite tricky as it was one of those narrow windy roads that are quite high up. I hadn't realised quite how high up we were. Dad thought it might have been a stag taking a glancing blow from the corner of our car. But there was nothing there. We both got out and looked, and for Dad, there was clearly nothing there, and whatever had been there had run off and was probably ok. Probably ok.

But whereas Dad's uncertainty and worry then ended after a brief and logical investigation, for me it was just starting.

I started to check the rough grass and heather at the side of the road and search behind the ferns. I repeated this several times, despite my dad repeatedly asking me to get in the car. I just kept looking again and again.

I even looked on the other side of the road too, just in case I had got it wrong, and the bump had actually happened on that side. And then once the other side of the road had been checked, those previous memories seemed to melt away and I felt compelled to repeat the process all over again. Then, when even **I** knew there was nothing there, I walked to the side of the road and looked down the steep grass slope.

I couldn't bear to think of a wounded animal in distress, dying somewhere. Because of us.

Then I felt a hand on my shoulder. "Jamie, we need to leave." And so I got in the car.

But as we drove away, all I could think of was this: was the animal a wounded cyclist? Had we killed someone? Was there someone dying in the grassy verge and we'd just driven off? And we would never know. And someone somewhere would be missing a father, or a mother, because of us.

Because of me.

Chapter 5
Mountain I

As they traversed the rocky outcrop that carpeted their path, they looked out.

Bursts of red, yellow and bronze peppered the landscape and the view was both sad and joyous. Both at once.

Beneath them, the land sloped down into the majestic crystalline loch. Above them, the mossy slopes eventually gave way to the rocky peaks and then to the dramatic sky above, a pale blue canvas, onto which swirls of ever-changing cloud had been painted. The clouds, sometimes pure and white, and sometimes ominously dark.

As Jamie looked at the loch, she was transfixed by how it reflected everything above to such a degree that it was hard to distinguish between the sky and the land and the water. Above was below and below was above.

And everything that was to come had already been seen before.

Dear Diary

OMG! This has been such a weird day!

School was crap. We've been studying Shakespeare. I like Shakespeare. Iona – she's always such a smarty pants – she says that she's read that Shakespeare, as we know him, never really existed. That he was actually a big posh English dude who didn't want to be associated with the scurrilous pastime of writing controversial plays, especially with Queen Elizabeth I being such a hot head! So, he created this whole persona of William Shakespeare, a little bit of a bumpkin from darkest Stratford, who came to London to make his fortune.

Iona, or probably Iona's dad, I reckon, thinks 'that Shakespeare' can't possibly have known all about the stuff he writes about – you know, politics, Greek myths, royalty, blah blah. Nowadays, you could probably blag all that stuff with a few Google searches.

Anyway, I like the idea of 'that Shakespeare' the best. He sounds cool, cooped up in his little London flat cranking out his plays. He just seemed to get stuff done.

My teacher said that there's a gap when we don't know anything about him for some seven years. Like nothing at all! But then he's referred to as being like a massive deal in London. The lost years. It's weird in a way. We call them lost years, but for 'him', he probably wasn't lost at all, just finding himself.

Finding my way.

So, we're doing 'A Midsummer Night's Dream', which is pretty cool, right? About living in a forest, with weird sprites and fairies. I would actually like that. As long as I could still play football. I used to love my mum telling me stories about fairies and stuff like that.

We've been writing essays, you know, using PEE language and all that stuff. 'In my opinion', 'my evidence for this', 'so in summary', blahdy blah. Imagine if you got people actually speaking like that?! Rhetorical question alert again. I kinda like rhetorical questions, you know.

The bell went for the end of the lesson and we were asked to hand in our essays. I was the last to hand mine in. Like I was dragging my feet. Like I didn't want to let it go.

To let go.

"Jamie. Will you nae hand it in? Please!"

So, I did. Why wouldn't I? I don't want people thinking I'm crazy. So, I have to stop saying that I am. I know it's only a diary, but you need standards still, don't you? Right? Maybe I use 'so' so much because I keep pausing. I pause all the time, to think, to check. And when you do that, well, I guess there's always a 'so' afterwards.

"Thank you."

His voice didn't sound very thankful. So, what's the point in that? Just don't say it. I left the classroom, but no sooner had I left than I wanted to go back. It suddenly occurred to me … had I written on the back of the essay, "Mr Thompson is a dick"? Maybe it was worse than that. I am sure you can imagine, I certainly can!

Like all the time.

So, I say to him, as he's packing up his stuff, "Sir, can I have my essay back?"

But instead of just saying, "Yeah, sure, here you go," he HAD to say, "Why would I give it you back, Little Missy?"

Little Missy!!!!! Seriously! OMG, no emoji can truly sum up my feelings at this point. I am literally lost for words.

I'm trying not to say 'so', so I'm not going to say it! Grrrrrrr!

"I just need it back, please."

Dear Diary

OMG, could I actually play well in one of these diary entries?!

I thought I could actually play football! Robbie said I could. Now I feel as if I can't even put one boot in front of the other without falling down!

So, we're at John Brown's pitches and we're training, getting ready for this Sunday, 'cos we're playing the boys. The boys U13s. They think they're going to beat us, 'cos they're boys. So, obviously, they'll beat us! Right? Even if they're younger and half of them look like they're nine, they'll still be expected to beat us.

'Cos we're girls. Right?

Boys are mostly solos, in my opinion. They dunnae play like a team. They might think they play like a team, but they dunnae. We've played so many boys' teams, always younger than us, but that's fine. I guess that makes sense. But to me, they just run around like little ants, trying to do fancy stepovers and trying to show how much better they are than us. What did my mum call that? Ego! That's it, ego. Whereas in my team we don't have so much ego.

I mean, people say I can play and I'm sure I can. Robbie says I can and that's good enough for me. Robbie will play for Celtic one day, I'm sure of it. But generally, I think we just play as a team. Nothing fancy. But we work hard and have got each other's back. And some of us, I guess, have got that bit extra to go past someone, to put the ball in the net. Finally. Or all of a sudden. Either will do.

We're huddled together at the side of the pitch, hoodies on. Bruce is going through what we're going to be doing. One of the other dads, Stuart, takes us through the warm-up. Stuart used to be in the RAF, so he knows what he's doing, unfortunately, as the girls hate doing planks and burpees!

After this, we do a drill to test our goalkeeper, Lindsay, and our shooting! Someone passes the ball to us from inside the eighteen-yard box and we're asked to smash it home! Halfway through the warm-up, I start to feel lousy. But not even lousy. Just blank. Like someone's turned off the lights. I didn't see it coming. I never do.

I never do.

I'm meant to have a good shot, a great shot sometimes. Maybe. Robbie comes in from the right and shoots with his left. I like to come in from my left and shoot with my right.

I come in from the left, the ball bumbles a bit, my boot goes back, I barely hit the ball.

"Jamie, you're nae even trying now. Go and play up the other end. Tell me when you've mastered actually kicking a ball."

I walk over to the side of the pitch. More of a trudge, I guess.

I stand there in the opposing penalty area. Alone. The faint sound of the girls calling out. The gruff, annoying voice of Bruce bursting through. But distant enough. I position the ball. I position myself and am just about to kick it when I get a tap on my shoulder.

"What's up with you?"

I turned around quickly. It was a man in his sixties.

"Where did ye come from?"

"I'm just helping out the team. What's wrong?"

"What do you mean what's wrong?"

"Well, you nae seem yerself. Don't worry about him. He's a jerk. Robbie told me."

"Robbie told you?"

"Aye."

Chapter 6
The Therapist

"Jamie?"

"Yes."

"I need to speak to you about something."

"Ok." Jamie stirred her chocolate cereal, trying to avoid eye contact with her dad. Her spoon drifted around the bowl, making a series of concentric circles. As each chocolate circle was formed in the milk, she watched it fade away, only to be replaced by the next and the next.

"Jamie? I said I need to speak to you about something."

Her spoon chinked on the side of the bowl. She looked at her dad.

"Aye, and I'm listening," she said, mildly piqued. *Why did people take so long to get to the point?*

"Well," her dad continued, "I think we need to think about you seeing someone, about how you are feeling a lot of the time. And about your checking. I was twenty minutes late for work the other day after I dropped you off. We didn't need to stop. It was just a pothole, Jamie. Just a wee bump in the road. But I can't keep being late for work. If I'm due at a meeting, well, it looks bad. And people talk."

"What do you mean, 'people talk'?!"

"Well, I just can't keep being late all the time. That's all."

"Ok," Jamie replied, further irritated.

But when she thought about it, it did make sense. He couldn't keep being late. It was only every so often at first and then only a few minutes late. But now it was pretty much during every journey and she was checking 'the scene' for much longer each time. She did concede that.

That it was getting worse.

"Well, anyway, I was just speaking vaguely about this sort of thing at the university."

Jamie was fully engaged now, but not in a good way.

"What do you mean, 'speaking vaguely about this sort of thing'? How can you vaguely talk about somebody getting in the car every day worrying that the car they are in has run someone over? How can you be vague about that?"

"I just said you might have a few issues that have risen again. Maybe since your mum died. And we do need to avoid you ... you know, the hospital. Again."

Mum. Jamie stopped stirring her cereal and stared at her dad. Stared through him.

"Aye," her dad went on. "Well, I've been suggested this guy. He's a hypnotherapist. He's very good, apparently."

Jamie turned her head to one side and looked at her dad wide-eyed.

"A hypnotherapist?! Seriously? Like a hypnotist?! What's he going to do? Turn me into a chicken? How's that going to help?"

"Well, Jamie," her dad said, folding up his newspaper and picking up his latte, "it's worth a go."

Jamie glared at him. She didn't like the fact he'd been talking about her. However vaguely. She wondered what else he'd told this person. Did they think she was nuts? Jamie thought that herself. Sometimes. A lot of the times.

Jamie was slumped in the car, lost in the music playing on the radio, eyes closed, wanting the journey to never end.

I don't want to go there, she thought. It's going to be a disaster. I don't want to be a chicken. She SO didn't like meeting new people for the first time, even new teachers. Never mind hypnotherapists in some strange part of Glasgow she'd never been to before.

Curiously, they did hit a pothole on the way there. Jamie pointed it out herself. She never asked her dad to stop though. Curiously.

They parked up in a revitalised part of the city. They got out of the car and walked to the enormous glass doors of the building. It was an industrial-looking complex that had obviously been a factory in a previous life. It was an odd mix of an original sandstone structure from the 1900s combined with modern flashes of chrome and glass. The car park had been constructed and shaped accordingly but then swept out into a wider post-industrial wilderness for as far as Jamie could see.

They walked through the unwelcoming glass doors, though their warm transparency was probably meant to be welcoming. Not for Jamie, though. She hated the doors.

Jamie took a sweet from the bowl on the counter in the sheened reception area and slumped down next to her dad. Feet planted. He perched nervously, checking the time.

The smart, pretty-looking lady in reception called them up and told them to go to floor 3.

They took the lift. Jamie hated lifts. Like a cold metallic prison. Maybe the unforgiving prison door would never open, and they'd be trapped there forever, condemned to a long, lingering death devoid of oxygen. And when would their listless corpses ever be found? *Possibly when the next person pressed the button for floor 3?*

Apart from that, though, she thought lifts were fine.

As they sat on another set of chrome chairs, the softly-spoken young man in reception told them that the hypnotherapist would be with them shortly. Relaxing, meditative music played in the background. Jamie hated this type of music. It made her feel the opposite. There was a strange smell in the air, some distant scent that was also meant to make her feel relaxed and at peace. This also failed.

Eventually, the therapist appeared. A tall man with coiffured hair and an accent which seemed half English and half American. Jamie didn't like him.

They went through to his treatment room. As Jamie was only fourteen, it was agreed that her dad would stay in on the session and sit at the back of the room.

Jamie sat down in the big, deep chair. Petrified. The man put a blanket on her. A bit weird. He then lowered the seat with his foot so Jamie was fully reclined. And fully relaxed and ready to receive his therapeutic input. Not.

"I want you to feel a golden glow in your head. And I want you to take this glow down your body. Down through your arms and through your hands, into your fingers."

The man went through a series of these well-rehearsed routines. And Jamie did not feel more relaxed. And she really did try.

"So, Jamie, I want you to imagine yourself sailing away on a boat. You are there ... drifting away ... the serene waters clipping away at the bows of your boat as you continue to drift through the lake to the horizon."

Jamie had always liked water and preferred this part of the 'therapy' to the counting down and the lift analogies, which made her feel claustrophobic. She didn't like lifts.

"And so, you are drifting through the waves, Jamie, at one with the world. Everything is fine with the world. Then the boat stops, Jamie. Tell me what you can see."

OMG, stop saying my name, Jamie thought. Stop being so annoying.

"I can't see anything. I'm on a boat. What do you think I can see? Just sea. Actually, nothing. I can see nothing. Is that ok?"

"Stop, Jamie! What can you see? Right now! Tell me now!"

"Nothing! Stop shouting at me!" she replied. She was crying.

"You're thinking too hard, Jamie. Stop thinking. What can you see?"

Wait, Jamie thought, how can I stop thinking? That's what I do, isn't it?

Everybody thinks.

With that, the master magician admitted defeat and, quickly whisking off the blanket, began pumping the chair back up to the upright position.

Dismissing Jamie and turning his attention to her dad, the man said, "I think we're done. It's not working. It happens."

Well, that's convenient. Thanks a lot.

"You can get your money back at reception."

They walked to the car in silence and drove home in silence.

Chapter 7
It's Off!

It was lunchtime. Robbie Blair was sitting by himself at one of the cafeteria tables. He was lost in his own world, dragging a fork with a chip on it around his plate, making seemingly meaningless patterns with the gravy. They probably meant something to Robbie.

"Hey!" Jamie said, putting her tray down and sitting on the plastic chair opposite him.

"Hey," he replied.

"You ok?"

"Aye. Same." Robbie was a man of few words. I say, man, he was still only fourteen. Just fourteen, in fact.

"I've got a big game coming up."

"Have you?" Robbie replied.

"Aye. A quarter-final against Paisley. They're top of the league.

Robbie nodded, his fork still drifting around the plate. His own private universe.

"You know I need to get fitter though. Will you run with me? Tonight?"

Robbie put his fork down. It clanked on the plate.

"Aye. 5 o'clock? Nice," Robbie said, standing up to leave the table.

Jamie smiled to herself.

"Well, thank you, Mr Mysterious. Same old Robbie Blair."

Same old Robbie Blair.

Jamie arrived at Robbie's house at 5:10pm. She had meant to be on time. She really had. But she kept stopping. And checking. And then stopping. And checking some more. The only time she carried on running was when a nice old man, returning from an allotment with his wheelbarrow, asked her if she was all right. It was like she wasn't on a pavement, but on a stage instead. And the spotlight was shining down on her. Only her. And the whole world was looking at her. And what she had done. What she was capable of.

"Are you ok?" the man asked, peering down at her.

He had kind eyes, Jamie thought. But why did old men have such big ears?

"Aye. I'm fine." She had to think quickly. What was she actually doing? "I lost something. Yeah, I lost something."

He looked at her and smiled. "Well, ok then. As long as you're ok."

"Thanks," Jamie said, raising herself to her feet.

"I hope you find it again," said the man as he went off on his way. *I hope you find it again.*

Robbie opened the door. They began their run. Robbie set the pace. Over the bridge, turn left down Dumbarton Road.

"How come you're always late?" Robbie asked as they ran along the road. Side by side.

"What do you mean?"

"What do I mean? I mean, why are you always late? I mean, it's nae big deal to me. I don't care. But other people might. Maybe."

"What d'ya mean, 'other people'? Has someone said something?"

"Noooo. No one's said anything. Honest. It's just..."

"Just ... what? Hang on. Stop!" Jamie shouted, bringing the run to an immediate halt.

Her right hand on her hip, her left hand stroking her slightly sweaty forehead, she said, "I don't know. But I think I might have left the gas on in my house. I cooked myself an egg before I came out."

"I'm sure you didn't."

"I'm sure I did."

"Ok."

Robbie looked at Jamie. She looked distressed. She was clearly not going to settle until she knew.

Really knew.

Robbie sensed what to say.

"No problem then, Jamie. We can run back to yours. We can check the cooker. Or, if you want, I can check it for you. I don't mind doing that."

Jamie instantly felt calm. Her heart stopped racing and her breathing became normal. It would be good if she could carry Robbie around everywhere she went. Then she would be ok. He would know.

He would know.

As they ran the one-and-a-half miles to Jamie's house, it started to rain. Sometimes, when she was playing football in the rain, she felt like giving up, like the weeping heavens above were just dragging her down, dragging her to a place where all her fight and resolve had washed away. But today, now, with Robbie by her side, she felt stronger. She knew the truth.

But did she?

They got to Jamie's home. Robbie dawdled around in the lounge, looking at the back page of a local newspaper, half expecting to see his hat-trick from last week against the Rangers Academy. Jamie went into the kitchen.

"Jamie? Are you done? Are you finished?"

"Aye, not quite. I'm just making sure, while I'm here, that we have milk for the morning. Else, we need to get some. Dad won't remember," Jamie lied.

She was nowhere near the fridge. Fridges weren't dangerous to Jamie. Fridges were fine – they kept things cool, nice and steady. Gas cookers, though – they were a nightmare. What if she left it on? What if the house exploded? Just as Dad came into the house.

"No, not quite. Not quite..."

"Well, ok..." Robbie replied, scanning through the 'nearly' back pages of the paper.

Surely he was in there somewhere? What else did he have to do? Three goals against their biggest rivals! Including a rainbow flick!

A couple of minutes passed. Robbie put the newspaper down on the lounge table. He noticed there were a few official letters for Jamie. They looked like hospital letters that he and his mum used to get about his leg.

In the end, Robbie poked his head into the kitchen. Jamie didn't know he was there. She was oblivious. Robbie watched her closely. She was scanning the hob. And scanning was the right word. Looking. Even checking wasn't enough.

It's never enough.

Yes, she was scanning. Up and down the hob controllers, whatever they were called. The top one, she was sure, WAS OFF. The second one, she was sure too. She was beginning to crack this! But then it occurred to her. Though she was pretty sure of the 'off-ness' of knob 2, she now wasn't so sure of knob 1. Knob 1 felt as 'on' as it could be. Back to knob 1. And so it went on. Jamie didn't even get as far as knob 3, never mind knob 4.

Robbie felt awkward, perched on the threshold, not knowing whether to interrupt her. In the end, he just spoke to break the interminable silence.

"Are you sure you're ok?"

Jamie swivelled around. Embarrassed. Robbie sensed her anxiety and joined her at the cooker. He quickly looked. Yes, looked. It was fine.

"Come on, Jamie. It's fine. We're good. You're good."

Jamie turned and looked at Robbie. Despite the unruly nature of his curls that cascaded across his blue and green eyes. Despite the randomness of THAT. Despite his scruffy jogging bottoms and his muddied Celtic shorts. Despite living only with his mum for most of his life, and despite his physical setbacks. Despite all of THAT, he just never doubted himself. He never doubted anything.

But Jamie, Jamie...

She doubted everything.

Chapter 8
The Keeper

It was training again. Jamie had had enough. Again.

She had been accused. Again. Of not trying.

"Go and practise at the other end of the pitch, Jamie. Get back to us when you're in the land of the living," snarled Bruce.

Jamie felt a cold, dark feeling of emptiness permeate her very core. She looked at him in disgust and walked off to the other side.

"What did you do wrong this time?" the voice came again. Like last time.

Jamie had just made it to the opposing penalty area. She turned to her right. No one was there. She was confused.

"He's not right. Don't get upset by him. People like that are angry for a reason. It's not you."

Jamie looked to her left. Nothing. She looked quickly to her right and saw a long face with bright, expressive eyes. He wore a cap that Jamie thought looked a little dated. He had a long, impressive nose that was one bus stop past being Roman perfect, but one bus stop short of being hooked. It was a strong nose.

Jamie stopped and put the ball under her boot.

"I do try. It's just ... sometimes I feel so dark, so empty. Like there's nothing there. A car with no petrol. That's what I feel like sometimes. And sometimes that feeling just comes out of the blue."

The man looked at Jamie.

"Yes. Even when there is a blue sky, Jamie, you can still get rough seas. Remember, nothing's perfect, Jamie."

Remembering the goal was netted, Jamie gravitated to the penalty spot, taking the ball with her. Almost hypnotically.

The man was there in front of her. His shirt outside his shorts, his old-fashioned workman-like boots bouncing on the barely discernible goal line. Jamie ran up to the ball and drew her foot back. The keeper looked at her. And winked.

"Robbie will help you. And Amy."

"Eh?"

She looked. But the keeper had disappeared. Gone. She went left anyway, as that was her plan. It smashed the back of the net. Top bins. High risk, but if it came off, it'd be unbeatable. All or nothing.

Jamie went to grab the ball from the net and walked back to the faded penalty spot. The man was nowhere to be seen. The sky was starting to darken, and the street lamps shadowing the pitch drifted into the hazy twilight.

Chapter 9
Mountain II

Robbie and Jamie ditched their bikes and clambered onto the icy path. The clear ice shattered beneath their trainers as they made their way up to the metal kissing gate that lay to the left.

A startled deer appeared suddenly and briefly stared at them before stumbling into the bracken on the other side of the path. Once through, they crunched their way over the frozen grass and then onward over the rocks that peppered the incline peeking through the snow.

Though the immediate landscape was afforded a generous dusting of snow, in the distance, they could see the peaks were capped with thick snow, save for a few craggy outcrops that retained their steely grey.

Behind the peaks lay a bleak, dramatic canvas, occasional glimmers of pure light giving way to soft greys and then ominous swirls of darker greys and blues.

As they trudged through the snow, with every weary step, Jamie felt like stopping. But Robbie Blair was having none of it.

"We will never stop, Jamie. You will not be defeated. You will never give in." Robbie looked at her with deep blue and green eyes that reached out into her soul.

And she knew she had to continue.

Chapter 10
OCD – Part One

"Jamie. You are going. And that's the end of it. It's booked. If the other one didn't work, well, maybe this one will."

Jamie pressed her head down on the table in the kitchen and started butting it lightly. Not out of any self-destructive desire, just because her mind was totally empty of anything else to do.

"Are you listening to me?"

Her dad's words echoed back and forth in the empty arena of her mind. It was either full, teeming with chaos, or a barren hall with barren walls.

Jamie sat in the leather chair, waiting for this second 'therapist' to throw a blanket over her, click his fingers and transport her to another time. She was waiting for the man to lose his temper with her, to feel he had failed, to push her out of the door without asking for a testimonial for his slick, but sickly, website.

The man was relaxed and sat with his legs crossed. Ready.

"Tell me why you are here."

Jamie paused. Waited.

The pause engulfed the room. The particles stretched out, pushing against the walls, tightening their grip on Jamie. She gulped and put a hand through her thick, flaming locks.

"I'm a bad person. Like, really bad. I'm evil."

As she said the last word, she looked at Dr Blythe. *What was he thinking? Did he even feel safe himself? In a room by himself with someone who was ... evil?*

But he just smiled.

"Ok then, Jamie. Tell me why you think you are evil."

"I can't stop thinking bad things. Evil things."

Jamie paused. "The worst things."

"Go on."

"Well. If I was near a cliff, I wouldn't be able to cope with it. I'd look over the edge and I'd just freak out. And think, what if ... what if I jumped off right now? Just like that. I'd be gone. The end of me."

The man nodded. "Pretty much."

Jamie went on.

"What if there was someone by me? What if I just pushed them? There. Just like that. Gone."

The man shrugged. Nodded.

"Yep, they'd be gone too. Pretty much."

Pretty much, Jamie thought. What was that supposed to mean? Was he not taking her seriously?

"So, what do you do then, to cope with these feelings?"

"I don't go near cliffs."

"Ok. Well, that makes sense. You don't run into many cliffs in Clydebank, so as long as you don't go on many seaside holidays, with other people, of course, well then you should be ok. You won't be in danger and anyone else you may find yourself near to will be safe too. Done."

Done?

So, that's the end of it. Right?

No. It's not the end of it, she thought. As if the man needed telling that. She was obviously there for a reason.

"Well, then, we're on another school trip. And we're all on this ferry to France. And it's all great at first. We're eating and laughing and talking about the next few days. Going to Paris and discussing the places we're going to visit. I didn't even feel like we were on a boat, in a way. But then someone suggested we go onto the deck. You know, to take in the views, get some sea air. I wasn't so sure. It filled me with dread. But I went with the others anyway. As we opened the door, the icy blast of the air smashed into my face and I felt a bit dizzy. We then walked onto the deck and made our way to the ... the rail. One of my friends stood by the stern and stretched out her arms dramatically. She closed her eyes and shouted out, 'Where are you, Jack?'

"It was funny. But I didn't know how she could be so relaxed. When she was so close to possible danger. I shuffled my feet a little closer; I gripped the rail tightly and looked over. I felt sick as I watched the roaring waves rise and crash against the side of the boat. Some people were looking at the horizon and a distant ship travelling the other way. Some looked at the seagulls circling the ship in the sky. But I just looked at the waves. The waves."

Jamie paused. The doctor said nothing.

"I wondered, if I fell in the water, would I survive? How long for?"

"But why would you end up in the water? You were enjoying the trip, weren't you? Laughing with your friends. Looking forward to the days ahead. It sounds great."

"Well, I might just throw myself in. Or I might..."

"What? Push someone else in?"

"Yeah. What if I did that? So, I walked away from everyone else. Then they'd be safe."

"Of course. Makes sense. So, that's them sorted. But what about you, Jamie? You can't walk away from yourself. Can you?"

Could she walk away from herself?

"Well, no." Jamie felt irked again. *What was he trying to do?* "So, I went back inside. And I never went outside again. I mean, I never went out on the deck again."

But in a way, maybe that was what she had meant to say. Perhaps she would prefer it if she never went outside again. She would be safe and everybody else would be safe too.

"Ok, so the cliff's gone."

"Cliff?!" Jamie was annoyed again. "What cliff? Why are you saying cliff?"

"Sorry, my fault. I think I was just thinking about your previous ... you know, story."

"Story? So, I'm telling stories now? This is real! This is how I feel. They're nae stories."

Dr Blythe looked at Jamie. Jamie looked at Dr Blythe.

"I know, Jamie."

Chapter 11
OCD – Part Two

When Jamie woke up, it wasn't with dread. For once. On this non-descript, drizzly Tuesday morning, when she opened her eyes, they snapped into focus.

A purpose.

After school, she was due to go and visit the therapist again. But instead of feeling dread, she was actually looking forward to it. She liked the man. Occasionally, he had annoyed her, but having thought about it, she felt he understood her and what she was attempting to say. And he was an expert in whatever she had, after all.

Whatever she had.

"You ok, love?" her dad asked, looking at her over his spectacles.

"Yeah. All good. I like him. I'm good."

I'm good.

Gosh! she thought. I sound like Robbie Blair!

Dr Blythe skipped down the spiralling stairs and pointed at Jamie dramatically. Jamie thought he was a bit like Dr Who.

"So, Jamie. You went back in the boat. Was that the end of it?"

Jamie looked at him.

"You know it's nae the end of it. Why are you asking that?"

"I'm sorry then."

Was he really sorry?

"Go on then."

Jamie composed herself.

Where would she go? Next. Was it a next? Was this a next type of story? Maybe.

"So, I'm struggling a bit at school too."

"Are there cliffs there, too, Jamie?"

This didn't irk Jamie. Because he hadn't said that. She had.

Jamie twisted her head to the left and noticed the laces on her Converse trainers. One of the loops was disproportionately larger than the other, like it could come undone. Has anyone seen a lace come undone? I mean like, really seen a lace come undone. The exact point. Jamie suddenly put her woolly hat on. Curls of auburn hair, tamed by the hat, flowed on either side of her pale face. Framing it.

"Yeah, at school... I've started asking for essays back."

"Why? Are they not good enough?"

"No, I think I've written stuff on them." Jamie squirmed.

"Stuff?"

"Like bad words. About the teacher. Mr So-and-So is a xxxx. Mrs So-and-So is a fat xxxx."

"Ok."

"And when I grab it back, I look at it. Well, not all of it, actually. Just the back of it. Where I haven't written anything. And I look at the blank page. I mean, really look. Without blinking once. But the more I stare, the harder I stare, the more I don't trust what I'm seeing. I can't look at the page as a whole; I have to look at the page in sections. And pretty much, as I scan down the page in sections, by the time I get halfway, I go back to the top because I feel I've missed something and don't trust what I've seen!"

"But what do you see, Jamie?"

"I think I see swear words. Bad words."

"But do you? Do you, Jamie?"

"In the end, I never get to the bottom of the page. And the teacher just grabs it back anyway."

"And have you? Have you got in trouble for swearing at your teacher, or calling the other teacher a fat xxxx?"

"No. I haven't." As Jamie replied, she clicked her fingers and tapped her head. Her voice changed and her heart calmed. "And then there was the knife thing."

"Knife thing?"

His casual response almost seemed at odds with the words Jamie had uttered. And, come to mention it, Jamie thought, did 'knife' really go with 'thing'? Shouldn't 'thing' belong with something that isn't really that important, almost a bit stupid? The bowling alley 'thing' – you know, when Hamish's trousers fell down as he was just about to bowl his final ball. That daft thing that we all remember. But a 'knife thing'?

"Go on."

"Well, one time, my mum was at the sink. She was washing up."

"Makes sense."

"Well, anyway, I was drying up. And I wasn't really thinking about what I was doing."

"But why would you think about it? You're helping with the washing up."

"But then I looked in my hand. There was a big knife."

"Which you were drying up. You get knives in kitchens. They're used for cutting stuff up."

"And it suddenly came to me. What if I took the knife and just hurt her? Hurt my mum. Real bad. Right now."

"Ok."

"And the more I thought about it, the more I thought I could actually do it. Right now."

"Right now?"

"Yeah. Right now."

"And did you?"

"Well. No. Of course, I didn't. But I could've."

"Aye. You could've. That's right. You could've. But you didn't. You didn't, Jamie. There's a big difference between thinking something and doing it. You think they're right next to each other. Like one bus stop apart. But in reality, they're worlds apart."

Worlds apart.

Mum.

Jamie hadn't thought about her for a while. Maybe she had blocked her out. But she was thinking about her now. Right now.

Jamie was back on the pavement. She was cross with her mum. Jamie could be cross. Real cross. Jamie could think mean things, too. Jamie was a bad person. Is a bad person. Her mum looked stressed.

"I haven't got time for this, Jamie. Really, I haven't."

Jamie knew that her mum was busy at work, and she was spending more and more time at her computer and the library. Often, Jamie would walk past her office and her mum would call out, "Amy, I understand you. I get you."

Who was Amy? A work colleague?

"OMG! There's always something. You just never get me. You get Amy, whoever she is. But you don't get me. Whoever I am."

And with that, Mum was gone.

That's why I'm here.

Chapter 12
OCD – Part Three

Jamie made herself comfortable. She sipped at her water and considered adjusting the laces on her battered Converse trainers. But left them.

"So, Jamie. I want to say three things. Firstly, I want to say I think you are doing well. I really do. I understand you. I get what you are saying. You have been very clear. And, in a way, I feel like I was there with you too."

"Secondly..." He took his glasses off and looked at Jamie intently. "Jamie, you have OCD."

"OC what?"

"OCD, Jamie. You have a form of obsessive compulsive disorder."

"But I thought that was people rearranging tins in the cupboard and not stepping over cracks in the pavement?"

"Aye. It can be. But you have another form of it. That's all. Yours is to do with thoughts. Not tins. But just like someone can't cope with the tins pointing different ways and feeling COMPELLED to turn them the right way, you can't cope with the thoughts that come into your head. Instead of letting them fly in your head and waiting for them to fly away again, you stare at them full-on. And that, Jamie, makes them want to stay longer. In your head."

Dr Robert Blythe continued. "You see, Jamie, you are not alone." He stared at her. "You really need to get this sorted, Jamie, before..."

"Before what?" Jamie was quick to pick up on the word 'before'. She was always quick to pick up on the smallest of things. Perhaps this was a plus point of having this OC...D?

"Listen to me. You just need to know that you are not alone. Every one of us, every single person on the planet who has ever existed, gets crazy thoughts in their heads at some point. Everyone. But whereas most people just accept them, and, like a bird, they fly in and then leave again, Jamie, you are so disturbed by them that you find it very difficult to let those thoughts go. And the more you think about how you really don't want them in your head, well, the more they hang on. They want you to be alarmed, Jamie. It's the fuel they need. Don't fuel the thoughts. Let them go. Just let them go."

Jamie listened, her eyes drinking in all of his thoughts. She liked the doctor's voice anyway and could have listened to anything he said. But these words. These words made total sense to her and, for a brief moment, she felt calmness and clarity in her mind. The stormy waters of her tempestuous thoughts eased and became the silvery loch of her dreams.

"Ok. I think I'm starting to get it," said Jamie, slowly beginning to smile, a faint smile, as if being roused from a hypnotic slumber.

"'Before'. What did you mean by 'before'?"

The doctor shuffled to the edge of his chair and, touching his stubbled chin, continued.

"I'm really sorry, Jamie, but I won't be able to see you anymore. I have been helping research post-traumatic stress disorder for quite a while, and an opportunity has arisen for me to go overseas and help victims of earthquakes. I am really sorry, Jamie, to let you down. I think you have been doing very well; I really do."

Jamie gulped and her eyes welled up. Why!!!?? Just when she thought she was getting to the bottom of her problems. Well, nearer anyway.

She felt let down. She sprang up out of her chair.

"Just forget it. I wish I'd never told you anything. It's been a waste of time!"

The doctor tried to answer her, but Jamie wasn't listening. His words were just abstract sound waves echoing around her mind.

Just sounds.

Chapter 13
Sleep

Two weeks later.

Her dad knocked on her bedroom door.

"Yes."

"Are you awake?"

"Yes."

"You can't stay there forever. In your room. You just can't, Jamie."

Jamie lay under her duvet. She didn't know whether it was night or day. They were both the same to her. She just felt numb. Devoid of all feelings. Good or bad. She just wanted to sleep. To escape.

She'd done this for days. And days. Now, those days were turning into weeks.

"Don't come in."

"Love, you can't stay there forever."

Jamie went back to sleep. Escaping.

Later on, Jamie's dad knocked at the door again.

"I've got to go to school today. There's a meeting."

Jamie understood. She understood school. She understood 'meeting'. But she didn't care. She was past caring. She just wanted to sleep. She sunk ever deeper into her duvet.

She waited for the door to shut. Then, she felt calmer. Just four walls, protected by her duvet. No harm could come to anyone.

She hadn't been sleeping. At all. She slept in the day when she should have been doing stuff. Something, anything. And then, at night, she couldn't sleep. And that's when she was scared the most.

At night. She'd lay there, looking up at the ceiling, her breath would become short, her heart would race. Please let me sleep, she would chant to herself. Why won't you let me sleep?

One time, she felt herself drifting off. At last. But then, suddenly, she was awake again. By the road. She can see the car coming. Coming ever nearer. And her mum is looking the other way. Jamie stares at the car. The car, coming ever nearer. Let her mum know. Tell her. But Jamie can't speak. She can't make a sound. Nothing. Do something! Touch her. Move her. Let her know. Somehow. But Jamie can't do anything. She's paralysed. Frozen in time. Stranded, fixed on her bed sheets, unable to move a muscle. With every sinew of her body, she tries to shout out, to move, give a sign. But nothing. Maybe some kind of barely audible grunt. Maybe. Wait, she can't even breathe. How long will it last? How long has it lasted?

And all the while, her mum looks at her, smiling. Her dark, bobbed hair unravelling around her pale, beautiful face. One last time.

And then, just like that, Jamie finds herself awake. Back. She thinks to herself, I don't want to sleep again.

Chapter 14
The Great Bukovski

And so it went on. Another week passed, and Jamie was still unable to go to school. Still unwilling to come out of her room even.

At one point, her tutor, Miss McAndrew, came to the house. Her dad invited her in. She was a pretty woman in her early thirties. She had straight, dark brown hair that was tied back in a neat ponytail. She looked efficient and organised, but there was also concern in her eyes. Jamie's dad could see that. He made her a cup of tea and they sat down in the lounge.

Jamie listened from her bedroom.

Miss McAndrew spoke first, her fingers forming a triangle under her chin.

"How's she been?"

Jamie listened by her door, the waves of sound travelling clearly through the wood.

How had she been? How was she?

Jamie waited. In the shadows.

A lower voice. Her dad. She couldn't hear much, to be honest. But maybe he didn't have a lot to say. He knew she wasn't well. Mentally. In his work at the university, he came across lots of people like Jamie. And especially when it came to sleep – his expertise – he knew the intricate mechanics that were contributing to her lack of sleep. He knew 'how' it was happening, but as to the 'why', he was less sure. Perhaps he didn't want to face it. Himself. Maybe, though he was an expert within the walls of the university, within the walls of his semi-detached house in Clydebank, he was just like everyone else. Just as clueless. On his own doorstep.

There was some more muttering and more hushed tones, but after the clarity of "How's she been?" the rest of the conversation was difficult to hear. Maybe she wasn't trying as hard to hear. Maybe there was nothing to hear. Nobody knew what to say.

That night, Jamie lay in her bed. Dreading sleep. She didn't want it to happen again. She didn't want to be there again. Stuck. Unable to move. Not again.

She got out of bed and looked out of her window. The sky was a deep blue and the full, gaping moon gazed down on her. A sprinkling of stars twinkled in the ethereal early morning light. The soft hazy beams from the street lamp streamed across the sky and Jamie could even imagine Robbie Blair running through the night on the pavement below. Maybe he was.

Wide awake, she switched her laptop on. She went to put her normal Minecraft music on. The simple, cascading melodies soothed her, filled the silence and, for a time, seemed to stop the bad thoughts coming in.

But just then, a thumbnail jumped out at her, staring her in the eyes: he said his name was Tom.

Curtains of long, brown, lived-in hair flowed down over his bearded face. He looked at her in the darkness, reached out with a thumbs-up and then took a swig from a green bottle. The label said Rolling Rock. It made her think of the Wild West. And his face – his face seemed like a cowboy, tough but wise. He knew things.

Jamie wrapped herself in her duvet and made the video full screen. He seemed to be in a garage, surrounded by speakers and guitar stuff. She didn't know about guitars or amplifiers – she didn't play an instrument or anything – but there was something there. Something here.

Something.

He started playing. Soft, beautiful melodies flowed out from his guitar. Warm and hazy. And with every note he played, his face expressed the emotion, the feeling of that note, etched into every fibre of his skin. The tune was like the most beautiful lullaby you could ever hear, and its warm, ethereal charm weaved its way around the walls of Jamie's bedroom. Jamie started to drift into a hazy sleep.

And then he talked.

"Good morning, kids!" he said, smiling.

What a nice smile he has, Jamie thought. It lit up the darkness of the room. Almost the opposite of the cowboy she saw initially. Perhaps people can be both.

He talked effortlessly. He didn't know it, but it sounded easy. It was easy. Jamie looked at the screen, transfixed. At last, she was thinking about something positive. At last, she was linked. Linked to the world. Not chained to a dark loop inside her head. Something nice, something warm.

And then he talked. He talked as if he was in the room with her. Not in a weird way. Just a nice way, like the wisest, most genuine person she could imagine. There was no gloss, no veneer. This was him. And then she slept. At last. And though she hadn't left her room, she had at least engaged with something, someone other than her own thoughts.

And that was a start.

Dear Diary

Dad knocked on my door. He said I can't stay in my room forever. He's right, of course. But I just cannae face the world yet. Not yet. I don't know how long I've been here really. The minutes, the hours, the days are just all melting into one.

I know Dad has arranged some sort of a meeting for me to attend, for us all to attend. OMG, can you imagine that? Will it be at school? With my tutor? OMG, imagine walking down the corridor, everyone looking at me. I can't. It's just too much! But he's right, it cannae go on forever...

Dad, bless him, has bought me a new bike. I kinda didn't need one, really. But I think he thought it might get me out of my room. And, well, it worked. He slipped a Post-it® under my door before he left for the university.

Go into the back garden.

So, I did. First time in two weeks, or maybe three. It was a beautiful bike. Gleaming in the sunlight. Brand new and begging to be ridden. So, you know what? I did. When I opened the side gate and wheeled it down the drive, I started to get nervous and my heart raced like it normally does. I thought about going back in. Every part of my body wanted to wheel it back into the garden and run back to my bedroom. To block out the world again. But a voice in my head just kept talking to me. And this time, not a bad voice, not a nasty voice. A nice voice.

Do it, Jamie! RIDE IT.

So, I did.

I went slowly at first. It was almost like I was on it for the first time! With Dad behind me, on some Christmas morning, pushing me so far, and then letting go...

Wow! It was beautiful. I didn't know, just didn't know that the world, everything about it, could feel so amazing. The simple things. It was perfect. The sky was blue. I could hear the birds. Again. But though it looked warm and summery, there was still a biting chill to the air, which felt good. It made me feel alive. And once I got into the countryside, I felt I was really motoring too. At one point on this big, long straight, I couldn't believe how quickly I was going. Like super quick. There was one cyclist who looked like a proper cyclist and I couldn't believe how quickly I reeled him in. But then I realised he was coming towards me ... Oops! I've definitely been cooped up too long!

When I walk around, I always feel out of sync somehow. Like everything's just too slow. And when I feel like that, I feel like I'm going to swear at any point. At any time. Especially at fat people. That sounds awful. How bad a person do I sound? But on the bike, I just felt right. Like finally, I was at the right speed.

That's it then! I'll just stay on my bike. Forever.

Chapter 15
Change of Scene

"Jamie," her dad said to her over breakfast.

"We've got the Easter holidays coming up, and I think you need a change of scene."

"Really?"

"There's a conference that I could do with attending and—"

"Yes? And...?" Jamie snapped.

"Well, I have been talking to Auntie Jackie. And, well, she suggested you go and stay with her over the Easter holidays. The Lake District air will be good for you."

"The air?!"

"Yes. And the change of scene."

Jamie didn't say anything. Just stared into the distance.

Her dad put her on the train and eventually, she arrived at the small station at the top of the town in the Lakes where her auntie Jackie lived. She got off the train with her suitcase and looked at the rows of granite roofs that lined the town. The rain pelted down relentlessly. Auntie Jackie waved and greeted her. She took Jamie back to her house – Jamie's home for the next two weeks!

On the way down to the house, her auntie tapped her on the shoulder.

"Do you still like reading? You used to. And writing. You used to write lovely stories when you were younger."

"Aye, sometimes. Why?" Jamie replied.

"Well, one of the last times you all stayed with me, your mum was working on something. She was always writing, especially when you had gone to bed. Well, the thing is, she left it here. And it's still here. It's a book, Jamie. I've read a bit of it. It's really good. I can see why she was drawn to this person. I think you might want to read it. It's about a lady called Amy, who lived over a hundred years ago. Anyway, I'll leave it for you. In your room."

Chapter 16
The Church

Jamie couldn't sleep. Again. She knew it wasn't late. Like 'late late'. Late was now dipping its toes into early. It was March, and hour by hour, minute by minute, second by second, moment by moment, the days were getting longer.

Jamie didn't know which she preferred: night or day. What a question, in a way! Sometimes, night was scary. Especially when she was younger, when Mum had just died.

The blind had been wound down most of the way, allowing glimmers of light to burst through the hazy, sleep-filled room. When Jamie woke, she did so with her mum's face gazing at her.

Dark brown hair, wavy. The sun's light catches each lock of hair as she looks over her pale face. Brown eyes. Glinting. When she smiles, Jamie is scooped up instantly into a small ball of happiness and taken to a swing in a play park both far away and here. Far away and here.

Jamie stepped out of the door and without thinking, went left down the street towards the church in the small Lake District town. She noticed the faint shadows of overnight rain that had left their marks on the pavement. Once over the bridge, Jamie was soon in the churchyard. Sensing spring, the daffodils had sprung up, almost overnight. Beacons of light, beacons of hope.

As Jamie approached the church door, she heard music. Cascading melodies, like waterfalls falling beautifully through her mind. She had never heard music like it before. The music was busy. Her mind was always busy, so it shouldn't work. Really. But it did. There were lots of notes, doing lots of things. But for Jamie, who thought lots of things, lots of the time, it helped. Maybe, even though there were lots of notes and lots of melodies, maybe they all belonged together and helped each other. And though the notes took different paths and journeys, the notes worked together and *were in tune.* They were working together.

Jamie creaked the door open. She peered through. It looked empty, so she walked in. On entering the church, she was immediately affected by the ceiling. Her eyes traced how the Norman stone pillars effortlessly became archways, which then spanned the tall, vaulted ceiling.

Echoes.

Chapter 17
The Painter – Part One

A knock came at the door. It was Auntie Jackie. "Jamie, are you ok?"

Jamie heard the knock. It reverberated around the walls of her room and around her head.

Are you ok?

Jamie clutched at the duvet and held her feet tight. She shut her eyes and withdrew into the darkness.

"Yes. I'm fine," she said, lying.

"It's just I haven't seen you for a while. You ok?"

Her shoulders came together, taking the burden off her head.

Gulping, she blurted out, "I'm fine. I'm going to go for a run. I'm looking forward to it."

Was she really looking forward to it? All she wanted to do was sleep and escape. Within. Not run. And escape.

Without.

"Well, ok," her auntie continued. "I'll see you later, young lady."

"Yeah, bye." Jamie pulled the duvet over her and embraced the warm, enclosed darkness.

Her phone went. The sound pierced the darkness of her mood and she immediately looked for her phone. It was Robbie. Her heart lifted.

"How are ya?"

"Not good. I feel crap. All the time. It's like the whole place is a big raincloud. Even worse than Clydebank. It's all so grey and I feel so grey. I cannae do anything."

"Just get up. Do something. Go for a run. Even if you dunnae feel like it."

"I feel crap. But thanks."

It was always good to hear from Robbie. She'd known Robbie Blair for three years now. They'd met on a deserted towpath in Clydebank, and from then on, they had been inseparable.

Go for a run.

Jamie was worried about leaving the room, never mind the house, never mind the street, never mind ... the unknown.

But then she thought for a moment, in that dark abyss under her duvet. Maybe she should go for a run. What good was it doing languishing, drowning in the depths of her own misery, when she could be out there? Doing something else. Pushing herself. She'd seen first-hand how Robbie had pushed himself. How she had pushed him.

Why could she not do it, too?

Jamie leant back on the front door and took a deep breath. She hadn't been outside for days. It felt weird being outside at all. She braced herself, took another breath, and started running. She didn't know where she was running. She just ran. She picked a point on the murky horizon and then just ran.

Before she knew it, she'd reached the top of the crag, as if Robbie was there, guiding her. Jamie bent over and drew a deep breath.

"Not bad," came the voice.

"Excuse me?" Jamie asked.

Towards the edge of the crag, perched on a foldaway chair, with an easel by his side, sat a bearded man, probably in his early fifties. He had a long face, an aquiline nose and a slightly distinguished look about him. He continued to gaze into the distance, into the unfurling canvas that stretched out before him.

"You came here the other day. You're improving. You're faster when you reach the top. And you're less tired when you get there."

Jamie was still taking in deep breaths.

"Well, I don't feel quicker, or fitter."

"You're getting quicker. Jamie, isn't it?"

"Aye, it is. But how do you know that?"

Jamie was getting used to strange things happening, spending so much time with Robbie Blair. But how could this man have known?

"'Cos it says it on the front of your top!" the man replied, laughing to himself.

"Oh, right!" Jamie said, laughing too. Now, she was starting to recover; she walked over to the painter.

"Can I look?" she asked.

"Yes, of course. But it's not finished yet. But you see, Jamie, they never are. And you have to just tell yourself they are finished, otherwise you would be here forever. Looking at the same canvas. Forever."

"That's deep," Jamie replied, still looking at the painting and then gazing out across the crag at the dramatic view that lay beyond her.

"Maybe," the man replied.

"Well, I've got to go back now," Jamie said. "It's been nice to meet you."

The man looked at her for the first time, his face softening.

"You take care of yourself, Jamie."

And with that, Jamie left the artist to his unfinished work and began the run back. Her auntie, who had just popped in on her lunch break, was pleased that Jamie had gone out for a run.

"You started your mum's book yet?"

The book, Jamie thought. Of course.

The book.

Dear Diary

OMG!

I know I say that a lot.

But it's just that a lot of the time, I don't feel like saying OMG. Well, not in a good way, anyway. I want to say it in a nice way.

Nice is ok, isn't it? They always say don't say 'nice', you're lazy! I get that, but to me, nice is ok, isn't it? It's good, isn't it? I get the idea of the 'nice police' knocking on your door, handcuffing you for rampant overuse of the adjective 'nice' when there's an abundance of other adjectives available. I get that.

And it's **that** OMG I want to use.

Not the other OMG. Not the one when the switch has been flicked, when it's all dark and I can't see any light. No light at all. No matter how much you tell me, I won't believe anything you say. Because I can't see you. I can hear you. But I can't see you. Please, not that OMG.

To be honest, I'm bored by my own voice. I'm sure there are a lot of people worse off than me. My mum used to work in special schools and she told me about some of the kids. Some of them couldn't do, like, anything. I'm not comparing myself to them. I'm not doing that. I don't know what I'm saying.

I just know my face is next to the window, lazily peeking its way through the ripples of thick curtain. Condensation's streaming down my face. I'm not in the past or the future. Just in the now. I'm looking out at the hazy night sky, streams of headlights melting with the rain and the glow of the street lamp.

I long to see you, Robbie.

Chapter 18
Amy – 1903

Amy never knew she wanted to be a footballer. Like, a proper footballer. It just seemed to happen. But why would she have wanted to be a footballer?

This was the early 1900s and it wasn't really the done thing for girls to run around a football pitch chasing a leather ball. How uncouth! How unladylike!

Amy had grown up in Govan, a deprived area across the Clyde from Glasgow. Like many people in the 19th century, both her sets of grandparents had made their way over from Ireland as a result of the potato famine. They had arrived separately in search of a new life. A new life in Scotland. Amy's parents were just babies when they made the journey, but she and her three brothers always felt connected to their Irish heritage. Not surprising, really, as they were surrounded by families who made the same journey and clung to their Irish songs and culture to remind them of 'home'.

They lived in a small terraced house, a stone's throw from the Govan shipyard, where her father had followed in his father's footsteps and found gainful employment. Her mother stayed at home.

Amy was a kind and sensitive child, but, in keeping with any girl being brought up with three brothers, she was happy to roll up her sleeves and get stuck into any of the street games that were taking place, including football. Some of the games would involve rival streets, and dozens of children of all shapes and sizes would join in. It would be quite a spectacle, seeing the throng of children chasing an old leather ball across the uneven cobbled streets of Govan. Amy looked quite the sight in her white pinafore dress, weaving her way past the boys, young and old. Some of the boys struggled with this, and a crafty, cowardly boot would be left out for her to trip over. Most of the time, she managed to avoid such attempts to bring her down, but occasionally, and more to do with her footwear than anything else, she'd be caught and brought to the ground.

Later on, when Amy would be nursing her grazed and bloodied knees, her mum would shake her head. "What are we going to do with you, Amy MacGregor? When are you going to learn? Girls aren't meant to play football."

But when her mum said this, she'd let out a wry smile. Amy knew what she meant.

Amy could read people, even from a young age.

And she was good at it.

Chapter 19
The Painter – Part Two

"Jamie, wake up!"

Jamie. Wake up.

Just before she opened her eyes, Jamie felt her face flattened across the starched sheet of the bed. In her mind, she clung to blankness, and then, when she opened her eyes, they embraced blankness further. She craved blankness. Nothingness.

"Jamie, wake up."

Again. Suddenly. Eyes open. Face to the side. Re-adjusting to the light, like a dog.

Jamie threw on her T-shirt, shorts and hoodie and flew down the stairs.

Like Robbie said. *Just run.*

At first, Jamie felt, heard and saw her feet landing each time on the cool, grey pavement. But then, with every stride, the footsteps drifted away in her mind's eye. To the point where she wasn't thinking at all, just doing. She ran over the bridge and headed towards the lake.

As the road bent to the left, she saw a metal kissing gate. She ran along the road, her eyes fixed on the gate. She tried so hard to look ahead, concentrate on the fixed moment, like Robbie did. But she wasn't Robbie. She was Jamie. And no matter how often she stood by Robbie or listened to Robbie, she wasn't Robbie. Sometimes, she thought if she could spend enough time with him, she could be more like him.

Could that happen? Was it possible?

But anyway, she carried on running along the verge, ash trees to her right. As much as she wanted to focus on one distilled, singular point, she gulped. As much as she wanted to do this, her mind raged against it.

Did I just punch someone? Did I just push someone into a car? Did I swear? Did I swear at a walker going past me dressed in orange? Did I tell them to get lost? Or worse? One after another. And another. And another.

Eventually, sometime later, Jamie made her way through the kissing gate. She scrambled through the fern-covered slopes and headed up to the craggy peak that she had reached two weeks before.

This time, he wasn't there. Jamie's feet felt the soft, crunchy grass of the hilltop. She could see they were high up. She could see. It was real. The sky swirled around in her eye. It was too much. Then, like an echo in her mind, the painter spoke again.

Jamie! Look at the sky. It's blue. But over there, it's grey. Over there, it's black.

Nothing is perfect, Jamie! Everything you look at and breathe in is imperfect. Nothing is perfect.

And, Jamie. You are enough.

Chapter 20
Amy – 1914 – The Team

It was just something to do at first. Something to occupy their break-times, keep the girls working as a team. But, slowly, it took off, as word spread that – wait for it – they were pretty good!

People started to come and watch them play.

Amy couldn't believe it when the supervisor at the Fairfields munitions factory said they were going to start a ladies' football team. When the whistle went for lunchtime, those girls who were interested were told to assemble in the main yard. A group of them had been playing for a while, but now it was becoming more official and people were taking more of an interest.

Jock stood there in the main yard, sleeves rolled up and his right foot, still wearing a work boot, resting on the brown leather ball.

"So, we're starting a team. We're gonna train, get you fit, have you playing as a team just like the men. Nae different. And then we're gonna play games. Like real games, real matches. There'll be other teams, just like yours. And crowds. So, who's in?"

Amy's hand was the first to go up. And she bounded forward.

"I'm Amy!" she said, offering her hand enthusiastically.

Jock shook her hand firmly.

"Pleased to meet you, Amy," Jock replied.

And with that, one after another came forward, eager to prove their worth on this new level playing field.

Chapter 21
The Visitor

"Jamie!" came the cry once more, followed by another knock on the door.

Jamie had somehow been oblivious to the previous barrage of knocks.

"Are you still alive?"

"Aye, yes, I think so."

Jamie's head felt fuzzy and unformed. She'd been playing Minecraft late into the night and was still in a virtual land far away, where she had built a log cabin beside a clear, turquoise lake that stretched out for as far as she could see.

When she was younger, her family had taken her to a friend of her dad's, who lived by a lake. She might have only been six or seven, but she could clearly remember walking down from the wooden porch of the man's house.

Was that actually true? Did he have a wooden porch? Or was that just Minecraft? What is a memory anyway? When you think about it.

She remembered dipping her toes into the icy waters. The blue sky unravelled endlessly above her. She gingerly inched forward through the moss-covered slate that covered the bottom of the lake. And then, past this, she found soft, yielding soil. She felt the lake deepen. Too cold. And then she stopped.

Just then, her dad's friend appeared like some kind of Greek god to her right, diving past her, superseding these incremental steps with one almighty, overarching dive. Jamie watched the muscular blonde-haired man cut his way through the shimmering mirror of water right to the furthest side of the lake and then return. In a matter of minutes. Whilst she was still wavering on the edge, this titan had jumped, conquered and returned. He shook the water from his broad frame and then returned to the house.

On his way past her, this Goliath peered down and, in a camp, theatrical voice, said, "It's better once you're in!"

Jamie made the last bit up, 'cos it was funny. But the rest of it was true.

Jamie rolled herself out of bed. She felt barely alive. Just dull. Black and white. Like a drawing on a page, a first draft. She stumbled into the shower. The door shut with a resounding thud. She liked the sound it made. She could be sure that it had happened.

She liked the shower. It was old-fashioned. She wasn't so sure how old showers actually were, but this looked old nonetheless. It had a great, big, unmoveable shower head that stared down at her.

In her mind, she was a female Wild West outlaw in a ramshackle, makeshift cabin and the shower head was an old beer barrel, whose bottom had been peppered with gun shots. Above the barrel, Jamie's outlaw friends poured warm water, heated from the open fire through the perforated metal.

That's what Jamie thought anyway.

There was just one cumbersome lever for directing both the flow of the water and the temperature. Jamie, still thinking about the glacial clarity of her childhood memory, thought that she'd had enough of Wild West outlaw heat and needed to go back almost full circle. Taking the lever, she moved it back as far as it would go in the other direction. Arctic cold.

She stood there braced. Robbie had talked about cold showers before and how they'd helped him. But this was the first time she'd experienced it. At first, she shuddered. She was now stepping further into the lake. Then she felt the unremitting pounding of the icy raindrops smashing their way into her mind. But not smashing as in creating chaos. The opposite. If only for a moment. The icy rain marched in and ordered her mind. Telling her what was important and what could be forgotten.

Jamie eventually peered out of Auntie Jackie's house and up the street.

Just run again. Like Robbie said. You've done it before. You can do it again. Stop thinking bad stuff's going to happen as soon as you leave the front door.

Jamie walked up the main street and turned right, taking herself over the old stone bridge and past the churchyard. She then followed the path up to the crag. Jamie had made up her mind. I'll go to the top. All in one.

She started off quick and assured. She was getting fitter, back to whatever her best was. Or could be.

Can you get back to something you have yet to achieve?

The sky looked beautiful, Jamie thought. Not perfect, like the man had said. Blue, clear but full of shadows too. Exactly as the man had said. Nothing is perfect.

The slate-blue peaks that gazed down at her from the churchyard were starting to become more defined, more achievable. As if her painter friend was adding more colour from his palette. But then she got a stitch and doubled over in pain. She stopped and wandered wearily to the rocky edge of the lane she'd been running up. Closing her eyes in exhaustion, she stumbled a little nearer the edge. She then opened her eyes and looked over the sheer drop.

Her mind spiralled out of control like a Spitfire doing multiple figures of eight across an all-encompassing sky. Jamie became disorientated and fell to the ground. There was only one thing on her mind. Her painter friend. Had she been talking to him? She felt like she had. But where was he? Had she pushed him off? Why would she do that? She searched nonetheless. Searching the blank canvas for something. Anything.

In the end, she just gave up, exhausted, and lay there on the mossy grass. Silent. At last.

Then came a tap on her shoulder.

"Jamie," came the voice.

Jamie opened her eyes. And she gazed. Squinting in the sunlight. It was Robbie. Robbie Blair.

Dear Diary

Robbie's back! Yay! Out of the blue. 'Out of the blue' ... another fronted adverbial phrase. Sometimes I hate it. An evil messenger ... for, like, the worst things, the worst news...

Out

Of

The

Blue

But yesterday was, like, the best of news. The best news ever.

Robbie. Robbie Blair was back!

This was what 'out of the blues' were meant to be!

Chapter 22
Old Friends

When they walked back to her auntie's house, he explained it.

"The thing is, Jamie. When I was really bad, like literally broken, you were there for me. You ran with me, timed me, you even got up at the crack of dawn and pulled a medicine ball under the water for me at the swimming pool."

Jamie chuckled to herself. It did seem crazy now she thought about it. She also thought she'd never heard Robbie Blair say so much. Or maybe it was a while since she'd

heard

anyone

say

anything.

Robbie went on.

"Your dad came around to speak to me and my maw. He said you might wanna see me, like I could help you ... and it's the holidays."

Jamie had forgotten that it was the Easter holidays. She seemed to have lost touch with everything like that. All the little details, lost in a bubble.

"Aye," she said, as they turned into the steep incline to her auntie's house.

She looked at him. "Aye."

Auntie Jackie was in the kitchen making lunch. Soup, maybe. Jamie suddenly felt really awkward, the two of them standing there in the shadows. But thankfully, her auntie helped her out.

"So, this is the famous Robbie Blair!" She was cutting up vegetables and adding them to the steaming pot.

Robbie nodded, smiling faintly.

"It's ok, love, I know all about Robbie. His mum dropped him off this morning while you were out. I was going to tell you about it this morning. But you'd gone."

She came over to them both and put her arm around Jamie. She patted Robbie's curly head.

"You're going to be ok, love. It's going to be ok, you know. Right then, young lady, show Robbie around the house and then lunch will be served!"

After lunch, Jamie sat with Robbie in the lounge. She suddenly felt very sleepy as she sank into the deep leather sofa.

"I've just been thinking, Robbie. How did you even know where I was?"

Robbie looked at her, scratching his mane of curls.

"You told me about your runs, didn't you? So I just kind of knew."

Just kind of knew.

Chapter 23
Amy – 1916 – Coming Home

They came slowly at first. But then they arrived in droves. A never-ending conveyor belt of wounded soldiers, scared soldiers. Traumatised men.

How different things seemed when Amy had joined everyone else to wave off the soldiers in the early days of the war. The streets were full of patriotic cheer. The men marched with boots braced for adventure, their eyes full of pride and jingoistic zeal. Some knowing they had to do the 'right' thing; others craving excitement.

Were these the same men returning? The look in their eyes. Amy could never forget that look. Haunted eyes, betraying the untold horrors they had seen. Would they ever see beauty in the world again?

One poor soul on Amy's ward was obsessed with washing his hands. Every few minutes he would ask Amy for a fresh bowl of water. He'd complain that his hands were dirty, but as far as Amy could see, they were perfectly clean. He had nice, gentle, graceful hands, Amy thought. More suited to playing the piano or painting a picture than brandishing a rifle on a battlefield or clenched in a muddy crater, digging into the earth, desperately holding onto a life that was slowly ebbing away.

Sometimes, he would look imploringly into Amy's eyes as she took his temperature.

"Will the blood ever disappear?" he'd ask.

"I'm sorry, I can't see any blood," she'd reply.

He would look at her, startled, frustrated. Why couldn't she see what he could see? His eyes, so wide, almost bursting. What had they seen? Amy dared not think of the sheer horror of what they would have witnessed. It was almost like his brain had been so overloaded with horror that he couldn't cope with seeing life any more.

It was worse at night. For all of them. That's when they relived it more. Like they were back there again.

"Don't go!" he called out to her one day when she was attending to her tasks, on her nightly rounds.

"Don't go!" he repeated. "I hate the nights. I'm back there again."

One time, when she went onto the ward, she couldn't see him at all. She was concerned he had wandered off and as Craiglockhart Hospital was such a complex arrangement of rooms and winding staircases, she was worried he might have fallen and was still on the floor somewhere, in the dark. Forgotten. But then she saw him, the whites of his startled eyes catching the light of her lantern. He was under the bed. Crouched.

"Oh, there you are, Jack!" Amy called out in a warm, comforting voice. "We thought you had vanished!"

"Don't let them send me back over! Don't let them, please, Amy!"

He started to cry. Amy sat on his bed and beckoned him to come out and sit with her. Her soothing voice and gentle hands eventually brought him to her side. It was like leading a frightened animal out of the darkness to safety. He put his head on the starched cotton of her aproned lap. And there he remained.

"Don't send me back."

"I won't," she said. But then she wondered. Could she promise that?

Soon, she found out that that was the idea. Fix them up and send them back. She couldn't believe what she was hearing. It was cruel. 'They' said it was just a physical problem and the men just needed to be 'patched up' and sent back. She even heard people suggest that some of the soldiers were being cowardly and were letting their country down. How could they say that? How could they even think that? How could anyone spend even a few minutes with these tortured souls and then reach those cruel conclusions? It was beyond her comprehension.

The main strategy to 'patch them up' was twofold and equally abhorrent to Amy MacGregor. Firstly, they were told to 'forget about it, old chap. Put it to the back of your mind'. Next, they were given something called electro-convulsive therapy, where they were plugged into a bewildering array of cables and wires and then had electricity sent through them from a big, ominous-looking machine. When Amy first saw the machine and the poor fellows attached to it, it sent shivers through her spine. And they called this therapy...

"Don't worry, old chap. We'll soon have you back there."

What was wrong with these people? Amy thought. How could they think that? What were they not seeing? There was surely another way.

Thankfully, though, she wasn't alone. One day, after wheeling one of her tormented friends to the electro-convulsive room, she could take no more. In the dusky light of the corridor, slumped in a creaking wicker chair, she began to weep. As she sobbed, she spoke to herself.

"Why are we doing this to them? Why are we adding to their trauma? Do the powers that be not see them at night? Why are we treating them like this?"

"I agree, my dear," came the voice.

Amy opened her teary eyes and saw a tall, bearded doctor looking down at her. He had angular features and a long, hooked nose.

"I completely agree. It's all wrong. They need to talk through the horrors they have seen. They cannot just be banished to a locked drawer, never to be seen or heard of again. It will always come out."

"Yes!" Amy cried out to the doctor. "Does all the bad stuff come to the fore at night? Is that why they are back 'there' again? At night?"

The doctor nodded sagely. "Yes, my dear. That's exactly when it comes out." He rested a comforting hand on her shoulder.

Amy looked at him with wide, imploring eyes.

"Why are we sending them back, Doctor? Why are we sending them back – to die a second time?"

His hand remained on her shoulder. He looked at her, sighed and then vanished.

Chapter 24
Amy – 1916 – The Hydra

One morning, after attending to her rounds, Amy was walking down one of the many spiralling staircases that were everywhere in Craiglockhart Hospital. She was tired, having worked through the night. And nights at Craiglockhart were particularly difficult.

Maybe difficult was the wrong word. Maybe. It was just all very sad. Some of the new nurses found it scary. But Amy, Amy felt sad. Felt sorry for the soldiers that they were going through this. And that they were going through it time and time and time again. A never-ending loop. And what was worse, she knew that for many staff in the hospital – well, the ones in charge – the main idea was to get the patients well enough to send them back to the trenches. Back to that hell that, in a way, they had never left. The idea, to Amy, was almost too awful to comprehend.

"Nurse," came the voice.

"Nurse," came the voice again.

Amy looked up. It was the tall, thin doctor from the other day, peering down at her.

"Oh, hello again. Sorry, Doctor, I was in a world of my own."

"You've been up all night, no doubt, judging by your eyes. Do you have five minutes?" he asked curtly.

"Aye. Sure I do," Amy replied.

"Then follow me."

Well, ok, she thought. He was quite abrupt, but at least she knew where she was with someone like that. She followed him down the winding corridor and into his office. It was quite a large room, full to the brim of papers. Papers everywhere. There was a large leather desk towards the side of the room, but Dr Brock bypassed it and headed over to the window, where two chairs were placed.

"Here, take a seat, nurse."

Amy sat on the leather chair and awkwardly looked out of the window. She could see the pond in the distance, flanked by trees. A swan suddenly drifted into view. How beautiful, how serene, Amy thought.

"You care for these men, don't you?" the doctor began.

Amy looked at him.

"Aye, Doctor. Of course. It's my job."

"Nurse. Forget your job. What I mean is, you care. You really care for the poor buggers, don't you? I can see it, and I've heard it. I've heard the way you talk to them. You really care."

Amy didn't know what to say and felt awkward. It showed in her face.

"Of course, I care. How could anyone not? Looking into their eyes, how could anyone not?"

"Quite," the doctor replied, his arms folded, his face still, his eyes fixed.

He bent down behind his chair and delved into a leather bag. He then produced a pamphlet. He straightened it out, dusted it off and proudly showed it to her.

"This is The Hydra!"

He was very animated. It was the first time she had seen him like this.

"Ok."

He continued. "It's going to be a newspaper ... a magazine, for the hospital, for the soldiers. It's their own space. A chance for them to write, to think, to do. Let's just get them doing things again. Interacting with the world. Instead of just … going round in circles."

Amy was enthused. What he said made total sense.

Get them doing stuff. Thinking stuff. Sports, days out, birdwatching, teaching children, acting in plays, writing poems. Remembering what it was to be alive. What it is to be alive!

"Aye. Sounds great, Doctor!"

"So, can I count you in, Nurse?"

Amy looked at him and smiled.

"Aye, you can. And you can call me Amy. If you want."

The doctor looked at her.

"Do you still play football, Amy? Maybe you can coach them? Think about it."

Chapter 25
Amy – The Trip – Part One

It was 10pm. Amy MacGregor was just starting her night shift. She looked at herself in the mirror, a little longer than normal.

Who am I?

Then, after tweaking her nurse's bonnet and tucking away some flyaway hair that was invading her pale, pretty face, she was ready to work. It was work, of course, but she didn't see it as work. More and more, she sensed that there was a reason she was there. At Craiglockhart Hospital. There was a reason: she understood the soldiers. She hadn't been to the Somme. She hadn't been anywhere. Just Scotland. And she certainly hadn't witnessed anything like the horrors these poor men had witnessed. There had been an explosion at the munitions factory, and that had shaken everyone up. But Amy had been outside in the workyard at the time, playing football.

The horrors. And there could be no more apt word to describe it. What they had gone through – the magnitude of it – the explosions, loud enough to shatter, literally shatter, their eardrums.

Dr Brock looked at Amy over his spectacles, which were perched on his hooked nose.

He was very precise and to the point. Some of the soldiers thought him too precise, even a little cold. But Amy didn't. She saw beyond that. Beyond the surface.

"Well, Amy. What they have been through will have been so unfathomably alien to their very being that all their beliefs about the world, their environment, everything they held dear and even took for granted, have been shaken to such a degree that they no longer relate to any of those things. There is a complete disconnect between who they are and the world. They just exist in an interminable loop where they perpetually relive the horrors of war."

Amy looked at the doctor.

"Aye, Doctor. And that's why they say to me sometimes that **it's never over**. Never over."

Dr Brock looked at her and nodded. He briefly turned away, but then, in a flash, turned sharply towards her.

"But here's the thing, Amy. It doesn't have to be like that. We need to teach the soldiers to believe again. To live again. They need to talk about their demons. But not in their sleep, not in the dead of night. And they need to be doing things. Not cooped up, stewing in their thoughts. Get them out there. Trying new things, trying old things. Connecting. Reconnecting with the world."

He was a clever man. He seemed on another level to everybody else Amy knew at the hospital or who she had ever met. She agreed with everything he said. She felt energised and ready to help.

Chapter 26
Amy – The Trip – Part Two

Amy MacGregor was so excited on the day of the first trip. Dr Brock referred to it as a 'cultural excursion', but that's what he was like – a little fussy. That was him all over, deeply intelligent and thoughtful, but packaged in a rather prickly, some would say cold, way. But Amy knew that, though his manner seemed cold on the surface, his heart was anything but cold. And to Amy, it was a trip! That night, on her rounds, she spoke about it to the soldiers, or the 'boys', as she referred to them.

She sat on Jack's bed and spoke to him, gently. Jack was under the bed, as usual. Occasionally, when he wasn't back in the trenches, he'd tell her he hid under his bed because he felt safe there. Protected. But usually, like tonight, he wouldn't say why he was doing it, because he was truly back 'there'. Sometimes, she would kneel and offer him a hand and a sympathetic smile. A simple act of kindness to reassure him he wasn't alone and that he was safe. But his wild, frightened eyes just looked right through Amy, as if she wasn't there at all.

"Back to it, men! As we were. Wait for the whistle. 3 – 2 – 1. Now!" he shouted, before covering his ears and flinging himself onto the cold hospital floor.

Amy knew he was back there. She placed her hand on the stricken man's forehead. She thought it was a good time to mention the trip.

"Jack. Tomorrow, we are all going on a trip."

Silence. Her words echoed across the ward like a stone skimming across a lake.

"It will be good, Jack. For all of us."

And with that, she neatly retraced her steps and made her way to the nurse's sleeping quarters.

The next morning, when Amy woke, the sun was streaming through her bedroom window, each ray bringing with it hope for the day ahead. Amy was convinced that the day would change everything. She just knew. And if they, the boys, couldn't see it, feel it, well, she would see it, feel it for them.

Dr Brock had written about the 'cultural excursions' in one of the editions of the new hospital magazine, The Hydra. He had asked the soldiers for their feedback. Some of them had then spoken to him about what they would like to do. For some of the others, it was more a case of speaking to them one to one, and Amy MacGregor was often the 'one' who spoke to them.

Amy had asked Jack where he would like to go. She made sure she spoke to him in the daytime. When he was still here.

Not there.

"Jack, we're going to start doing some trips away from the hospital. Where would you like to go, Jack? Your choice. What do you enjoy?"

Amy's voice was gentle and kind. But this was no act. You see, she was gentle and kind. When she smiled, it was because she was genuinely happy or she genuinely cared. And another thing. When she smiled, her eyes smiled too. There was nothing false about Amy MacGregor.

Chapter 27
Amy – The Trip – Part Three

Jack was lying on the grassy verge. It was a road, or maybe a path or perhaps both, at some time or another. The near side was bordered by a neighbouring field and the far side edged into a coppice of hawthorn trees. And then, through the coppice, you could just about see a green, rolling meadow rising slightly to the horizon. A pleasant, almond-like scent filled the morning air. But it was not pleasant for Jack. None of it was pleasant for Jack. It was like he was underneath his bed again. The whites of his eyes staring out. Staring through Amy. Where was he? Was he back? There?

"Always forward. Keep going forward!" he shouted as he lay on the grass, squinting into the sunlight.

Amy knelt by him and stroked his forehead. She told him where he was and that she was there for him. She always did her best, without apparently knowing too much of the inner psyche of the human mind. But she was kind and understood people. And sometimes kindness itself is enough. More than enough. She was then joined by Dr Brock, whose angular face looked down at them both.

"What is it, Jack? What can you see?"

Jack continued.

"7:30. It's time! It'll be easy, they say. We'll just walk in and take it. This time. Come on! Forward! Keep going forward!"

Dr Brock bent down and looked at Jack.

"But it wasn't easy, was it, Jack? Even so, you are here, Jack. You got through it."

And with that, Jack closed his eyes and almost fell asleep there on the grassy path, Amy still stroking his forehead. A blackbird suddenly landed by them and peered inquisitively at Jack's face, his expression for once at peace.

Later in the morning, the group reached Cartleston Hall, their planned destination. It was a Tudor manor house, one of the last surviving of its kind. Dr Brock thought it would be an interesting place to bring the men. Interesting, scenic, thought-provoking.

"You know, Amy. Just get them talking wherever they are. Whenever they are ready. But in the day, when the sun is shining, the birds are singing. Talk about it then. When they are doing things. Otherwise, they'll just keep it all in the same place and their memories will forever haunt them. An endless film forever playing out, in the dead of night. Always in the dead of night."

"I understand, Doctor."

He smiled. "I know you do, Amy."

As they stood at the foot of the extensive steps that led to the front entrance of the house, Amy gazed at the undulating, green lawn that stretched out before them.

Reaching into her bag, she produced a football.

Dr Brock laughed to himself. She is a footballer after all, he thought.

Her face lit up. She, too, was back. Cradling the brown leather next to the starched linen of her nurse's uniform, Amy shouted to the soldiers. To the men. To the boys.

"Come on then, let's see what you've got! Who can get it off me?" she teased as she ran onto the freshly mown grass. The pitch.

Jack stood there, hands on his hips, his thumbs perched gingerly behind his braces. Looking. What was she doing?

And then. And then he smiled. Amy had never seen him smile before. And his smile lit up the day. As Jack ran onto the grass, throwing his cap to the heavens, others followed in his wake. Smiles and laughter filled the air as the men tried their best to get the ball off Amy.

She danced and weaved her way across the grass, effortlessly deceiving all who dared to take the ball from her. She came towards Jack, her eyes focused, determined. She then came to a halt, dropped her shoulder to the left and then exploded to the right. But Jack was wise to the move and brought her merry dance to a strong, resounding finish. And, in the process, he literally swept the slight figure of Amy MacGregor into the air. But as she prepared for a heavy landing on the lawn, Jack caught her in mid-air, whilst controlling the ball with his right foot.

"You're good," Jack told her in his heavy Brummie accent.

"Thanks," Amy replied, laughing, as she got to her feet.

"I was very good. Once."

When the football was over, the group entered the house. Swamped by the sweeping grandeur of the hallway, the awestruck men slowly, cautiously looked around, taking it all in. Amy looked at them all, standing on the gleaming black and white tiles of the extensive floor, like helpless pawns on a giant chessboard, awaiting their next move. And in a way, they were.

"Dear me, Doctor. The thought of them going back to the trenches … it's almost too much to bear."

Dr Brock put his hand on Amy's shoulder.

"We are not in control of that, dear Amy. Sadly, that is for the powers that be to decide. All we can do is help them the best we can. Teach them to live their lives the best they can, and help them remember the things they once loved and the lives they once lived. Get them out of themselves, Amy. Get them doing things. Like I have always said, old things and new things. Doing things. Because that's the best medicine of all."

Amy looked at the doctor and smiled.

Yes. That's it!

Chapter 28
Amy – Into the Night

The next night, Amy was doing her usual rounds. She hadn't seen Jack that day. She was desperate to see him. To talk to him about the trip. She'd thought of nothing else. In a selfish way, she was hoping that he was still awake, even though it was almost always a bad thing to see that he was awake in the dead of night.

All was still on the ward. In the star-crossed sky outside, the moon gazed down and comforting beams of light drifted through the large Victorian windows, casting long shadows across the cold tiled floor. As usual, Jack's bed was perfectly made with military precision. Empty. Amy bent down to see if she could see Jack's haunted face.

"He's not there, you know," came a voice.

Amy turned around, almost embarrassed. Why though? She was just doing her job, after all. The voice came again.

"Yes, he's not there. I know you're looking for him." The man was reclined in his bed, smoking his pipe. He had pale, refined features. His voice pierced the darkness.

Amy stuttered. "Well, it's just that—"

The man continued, oblivious to Amy's stunted attempt at an explanation. Though there was really nothing to explain. On the surface.

Pipe smoke drifted in the air, creating an almost ethereal glow around him.

"Yes, he went out a while ago."

"Out?"

"Yes, out. He didn't say where. But he doesn't say much at all. So, no difference there. Well, there you go. Something to go on at least. Good night, Nurse."

And with that, the man stopped talking and began writing in his notepad in the dusky light. Lost in his thoughts.

When Amy had finished her round, she checked the time on her watch and returned to the nurses' quarters. Her shift had now finished. She usually stayed longer, always ready to listen. That was always more important than clocking in and out according to designated shift times.

But what of Jack? Where was he? Out? Her mind, and indeed her heart, began to race a little. And then a lot.

Preoccupied only with thoughts of Jack and finding him, Amy made her way down the many staircases and outside into the night. But which way should she go? Where to start? It was cold. She tightened her nurse's cape and, as she did so, an owl flew past her. As she looked around for clues, she noticed the buttressed outline of the hospital, silhouetted against the moonlit sky. She moved away from the hospital and down to the pond. She could see the moon gazing back at her in the clear, still waters. She would often come down to the water's edge with the soldiers in the day. But she had never stared into its ripples at midnight.

Amy moved past the pond and made her way through a gap in the perfectly symmetrical hedge that separated her from the next stretch of the garden. She then turned left and headed across a gravel path leading away from Craiglockhart Hospital.

Halfway along, Amy saw a small gate and another path winding away through some trees. She didn't know why, but after lighting her lantern, she felt compelled to follow the path. Onward she went. Once through the trees, which she was glad about, she found herself on another stony path. Though she had been at the hospital for six months, it suddenly occurred to her she had absolutely no idea where she was.

But just then, she noticed, just ahead of her, there just there, a building she had never seen before. There in the night sky, as if it had just beamed into view. Out of nowhere. But why was she drawn to it?

Amy glided over the remaining part of the path that led to the side of the building. With her lantern held aloft, and further aided by the moon, Amy could see that the exterior was made up of a series of beams almost in the style of a medieval building. She looked down and noticed she was now beside a door. A shaft of light came from a gap at the bottom. Slowly, she pressed down on the iron latch and opened it.

It was not what she had been expecting. It was a brightly lit room, a bit like a gym. The floor was made of small interlocking wooden planks. The walls were white and a series of red lines marked out some kind of boundary. And a man stood there in the centre of it all. Lost in his thoughts.

"Jack?!" Amy called out.

The man turned around.

"Amy?!"

Amy's eyes lit up when she saw him. He came over to her. And she could see now he had a football with him. He was dressed in military trousers and a white shirt, sleeves rolled up. He was strong and powerful, standing there in front of her. She hadn't noticed before. His short dark hair glowed a little in the light and his brown eyes twinkled rather than ached with sadness.

"I didn't realise this was here, Amy. I found it here a few days ago. I think it's called a squash court. You're meant to hit a ball on here. With rackets. But to me, it's my little training pitch."

As he talked, he flicked the ball between his feet, into the air and then started juggling it, all the time looking only at Amy. He was at one with the ball.

"Did you play football in England? Before it started? For a team?"

He kept the ball in flight the whole time, with hypnotic precision. Well, hypnotic for Amy anyway.

"Yes, I did, Amy," Jack continued. "Birmingham's best. Aston Villa."

Amy was stood transfixed. She had played at a very good level herself. But, as was her wont, she was disinclined to push forward her own glories. She knew what she had accomplished. And that was enough. In any case, he had commented on her skills during the trip.

He came closer to her. Focusing on her. Completely.

"I hadn't felt like playing football, Amy. Just standing on a pitch, well, it made me feel like I was back there. On the field. The battlefield. But when I stumbled across this place, it just immediately felt like a magical room. Away from the war. Just me and a ball. And maybe, just maybe, I could be like I was. Before."

But then, flicking the ball into the air and ingeniously trapping it on his neck, Jack called out.

"Come on then, Amy! Come and get the ball off me if you can. You're a great player, Amy. I could see that the other day!"

And with that, Amy MacGregor was back too! And for hours, they danced around the court, chasing a ball. A nurse and a soldier. On a squash court. One hundred years ago.

Chapter 29
Mountain III

Making their way up the gentle slopes, Jamie remarked to Robbie how mild it was.

"Aye," Robbie said.

But Robbie also knew, from his conversations with his great-great uncle Fred, that spring could be highly unpredictable. Just when you thought that winter had been laid to rest and spring was here, the temperature would plunge, and you would be back in the icy cold of winter. Once again.

As they marched on, the smell of burning heather pervaded the air. This was a sign of impending spring: out with the old and in with the new.

Further on, and into the small copse that led to a flowing stream, Jamie noticed the snowdrops that had burst into life during recent days. Spring really was here.

Jamie felt strong in her stride. Previously, she'd have worried about each step and wouldn't have been able to face looking forward. Only back. Robbie would've walked ahead, and, sometimes, though he was always there for her, she'd have felt herself lagging.

But not today. And, though there would be times when the distance between them would lengthen again, more often than not, she would be near him. In his wake. Trying to think more like him.

Chapter 30
The Court – Part One

Whilst out running one morning, Robbie noticed Jamie was keeping up with him now, even when he injected the runs with some interval training or extra effort. Basically, Robbie would suddenly stop running and then explode into life again. Sometimes he would walk, sometimes he would come to a complete stop.

"The thing is," he told her, "I mustn't know what I'm going to do, otherwise I'll prepare for it and it just won't be realistic. Anything could happen in a match. So, my runs, as well as being hard work, should be unpredictable."

"Ah, ok. Thanks," replied Jamie, perhaps a tad sarcastically.

Robbie smiled to himself.

With this in mind, on today's run, as they came over the stony bridge and past the churchyard, instead of heading back towards the town centre, on a whim, Robbie took a right turn and headed out of town. After half a mile, they took another left, again on a whim, and then about a quarter of a mile later, they took a right turn, which brought them to a particularly steep and narrow road.

"Come on, Jamie. This will be good for an effort. One more push before we make our way home. You can rest there and we can play Monopoly this afternoon."

"Well, don't you know how to live big? Go on then!" she called out, trying to get a little closer to Robbie, who had already bolted like a racehorse galloping towards the finishing line.

The lane veered to the right and arrived at a small collection of buildings. There, they stopped. Robbie could hear the fast-flowing brook, which never seemed too far away. Jamie sometimes felt as if the brook followed them on their runs.

Robbie silently turned right to trace where the flowing waters were hiding.

"Shouldn't we be going back now? It'll be getting dark soon," said Jamie, ever the cautious one.

Robbie was lost in his own world.

"Aye. In a minute. I just want to see where this lane takes us."

They followed the narrow tree-lined lane, which wound its way down to what seemed like an old farm building. The building had been done up, painted white. As they made their way towards it, the feisty waters of the brook were now only slightly below them.

"Wait. What's that noise?" Robbie asked.

"What noise?"

"That noise."

They could hear a thud through the wall, as if something was being hit against it. There it was again. Thud. And again. They then made their way down the gravel path towards what seemed to be the entrance to this mysterious building, hiding in the early evening dusk.

As if in a trance, they peeped through the glass-fronted door. They could see two men running around a wooden floor in some kind of court and they could see this because the back wall of the court was made of glass.

After a particularly long rally, one of the men, seeing the gawping strangers by the door, came off the court to let them in.

"Come in," he said, placing a towel around his neck.

Robbie and Jamie followed him in.

"Thanks. Is this squash?" Robbie asked.

"Maybe," he replied, now sitting on a black faux leather chair nearby. "Sometimes I wonder. But yes, it's squash. You guys lost? I suppose we are a bit off the beaten track," he said, chuckling to himself.

The other man, who was wider than his opponent, came and sat down.

"Not lost. But, technically, we don't really know where we are. I've seen it before," continued Robbie, pointing at the court, "like on YouTube. But I've nae played before."

Jamie, standing back, was impressed by how easy Robbie found it to talk to a complete stranger. She largely found encounters like this difficult. Maybe it was a by-product of going off and about on his many runs and strange training routines. Just getting out and about, amongst it. Immersed in life.

"Do you want to have a go?"

Jamie suddenly sprang into life, from the shadows.

"Can we? Can we really? But we have nae got rackets or anything."

"Well, you look sporty enough. Give your trainers a bit of a wipe." And, diving into a box of old rackets and grabbing a couple, he added, "Here you are."

"Thanks," they both said.

"Come on," said the man, "I'll give you some pointers."

They dutifully followed the man onto the court. He shut the glass door and banged the ball a few times with his racket, perhaps to inject life into it again.

The man began talking, and Jamie noticed how his words echoed in the strange white enclosed room they now found themselves in. How strange, Jamie thought. Only a few minutes ago, they'd been lost on a secret path near a babbling brook, and now they were standing in a strange room talking to a man about squash. Perhaps if you are open to opportunities, these things happen?

"So, how to grip the racket. It's just like shaking someone's hand."

He demonstrated how and they both carefully copied him, using their own rackets.

"Now, the forehand. You both right-handed?"

Jamie nodded.

"Aye, I'm left-footed. But I'm right-handed," Robbie told the man.

"You're a footballer then?"

"Aye," replied Robbie, before adding, "we both are."

Jamie tried to mask her awkward smile by emulating the man's grip on the racket. She stared intently at her hand and compared her grip to his.

The man came over to them and, jutting his jaw, cast his eyes upon their attempts. He took his hand off the racket and pinched his index finger with his thumb.

"Remember to lead with these," he went on. "It's like skimming a stone," he said, demonstrating the motion.

This hit home with Robbie, who nodded. He'd spent time skimming stones during his many runs, whenever he found himself on the banks of a loch or a river.

The man then performed a succession of forehand drives, drilling the ball low and hard against the front wall, one after another, his racket up and ready each time, his shoulder turning like a coiled spring ready to unleash.

"Wow!" Jamie remarked. "You hit it so hard!"

The man laughed. "Right then. Your turn."

"Well, ok then," Jamie replied.

Robbie noticed how she was speaking more now, slowly coming out of herself.

The man got them to stand in the middle of the court – the 'T' – as he called it. He stood behind them, facing the back right-hand corner.

"Right then. Start with your racket up, not down here like a broom. I'm just going to give you a nice, easy feed, and I want you to hit it back to me. Simples!"

Robbie went first. He was almost too quick, arriving at the ball sooner than he envisioned. He hit it cleanly enough, despite having to adjust his stride, quickly and intuitively, just before he made contact.

"Hey, not bad! Not bad at all," called out the man.

Robbie bounced away and ran to the back of the line, his racket up. Ready.

Amazing, the man thought. Week after week, he coached juniors and always had to shout at them to run back to join the line, to get their rackets up early, but here was this complete stranger who had just breezed in from nowhere and was doing it all without needing to be reminded.

Jamie was next. Her face was the embodiment of concentration as she looked at the coach. Ready.

"Try not to get too close. Stay a racket away."

The man served up the ball. To Jamie, it was as if it was all happening in slow motion. She followed the ball with her eye. Her racket up, as the man had instructed. She'd noticed how Robbie had got there too quick and too close. As the ball hit the front wall, she bounced swiftly from the 'T', but then slowed as she approached the ball. Her racket still up, she turned her shoulders, a racket length away from the ball and then struck it. It made a pleasing thump but with a twang of strings. The ball hit

the front wall about halfway up and carried on its clear and direct line to
the back of the court. Straight to the man who had become their coach.
Once she'd seen the ball reach its destination, Jamie bounced back away
from the shot and ran back to join Robbie.

The coach flipped the ball up and caught it with his racket, cushioning
it in the air and bringing it down to his hand.

"Amazing," he said. "You've both just hit one shot. And immediately,
I can see you are both naturals. Amazing!" he said, shaking his head in
disbelief.

They carried on playing with the coach for about fifteen minutes
and then had a game between themselves. Without his instructions and
guidance, their technique deteriorated a little and it became more a bit of
fun. But in those early moments on court with the coach, they had both
shown enough potential to have made a big impression on him. Later
on, in the pub, he would be talking about these two strangers who had
come his way that night.

When Robbie left the court to go and get a drink of water, Jamie was
left alone on the court, this secret stage that seemed so divorced from
the outside world. How comfortable she felt, just being there. How safe,
and how inspired. The stream still trickled by, of course, but the clocks
had stopped for her. All the random chaos of her unbridled mind had
been distilled to one singular thought. One vision. One objective. One
moment.

On their way back home (Auntie Jackie's place was starting to feel like that now), as they cruised across the stony bridge and past the churchyard, Jamie said to Robbie, "Do you know what?"

"What's that?"

"I like squash."

"Aye, it was good. He was a nice guy."

"I mean, I really like it. I felt safe and in the moment. And inspired. Like you do on a football pitch. Maybe it could help me. You know, get out there again."

Robbie looked at her. He nodded. He understood Jamie. He could see that there had been a change.

Her eyes lit up the darkness, whereas before, sometimes, they were the darkness.

Chapter 31
The Court – Part Two

Jamie couldn't sleep. Literally, that was an understatement. She was bolt upright, staring at the ceiling. Staring at nothing. Feeling nothing. In an instant, she jumped out of bed. She had no idea what the time was. When she peered out of the condensation clinging to the window, she could tell it was either still late or very early.

She had a thought. And for most people this would have been an odd thought, but Jamie was used to odd thoughts, so this was one of her more normal ones.

"I want to play squash! That's what Amy would do! And that's what I will do. Today. Thanks, Mum!" It felt good saying, 'Thanks, Mum.'

Within seconds, she had changed into her sports kit and was ready to go. Just got to grab Robbie now. Or wake him, at least.

The floorboards creaked, despite her best efforts to silence the ageing bones of the house.

She knocked. Their special knock. The one only they knew. Nothing. Even maverick heroes need to sleep...

She repeated the knock. Eventually, she drew a response.

"Aye. What is it?"

"It's me. I wanna go and play squash."

"Seriously! What are you talking about?! Squash! It's the middle of the night. The middle of the night!"

"You should be used to it! Or have you forgotten?" Jamie replied. Her toes ground into the deep pile carpet of the hallway.

"Well, ok then," came Robbie's final reply. Eventually.

Within five minutes, the door opened and Robbie Blair was ready. Hoodie, curls creeping out when allowed, white shorts, white socks ruffled down.

"Let's do it," he said.

It was still dark. The stars were still shining. They started at a steady pace, turning left at the end of the road, then a sharp right and then over the bridge. Jamie glanced at the graveyard as they did so. Graveyard. What a horribly depressing word, she thought. 'Grave' was bad enough. But 'yard' wasn't much better. Graveyard. She was glad she was running and wasn't in a graveyard.

She looked up. Though it only seemed a matter of minutes later, it was as if the night was opening up now and the darkness was mellowing in her eyes. In fact, the more she looked at the sky, the less dark it seemed. The darker tones at the top of the canvas moved seamlessly into lighter tones. This continued until the sky became a mellow, bronzed glow, a backdrop to the silhouetted crags and peaks that framed the stone town below.

"Come on!" Robbie barked. "I cannae keep stopping."

"Sorry," Jamie replied, getting going again. She might have said, "I'd forgotten how beautiful the sky is at night." But she didn't. She was embarrassed. But she should have said it. It was Robbie Blair, after all.

Eventually, Jamie heard the sound of the stream and knew they were near. She half-closed her eyes in the twilight and let the rush of the water navigate her way. They followed the stream down to the club. Streams and rivers continue to do their business, say their piece, whatever time of day.

As the path veered down, Jamie could see the white stony wall of the club. And it's funny, she thought, she hadn't done any checking during this run. Yeah, a bit of stopping to take in some beauty. But no checking. No random stopping to check if she had pushed anyone into the road. No dodging the cracks of the pavement to maintain the safety of her immediate friends and family. No checking at all. Just in the flow. Accepting who she was and running with it.

Just enjoy being in the now, Jamie. In the moment, the voice said.

Jamie opened the door with the fob that the coach had given them the previous day. He said they could use it for as long as they were in the area. Robbie made his way over to the corner of the gym behind the court and started stretching.

Jamie peered around the deserted club. She was comforted by the lack of people. She liked empty places. Sometimes, she liked to imagine she was in a big, empty French supermarket. Devoid of people, wandering around the aisles like a lost supermarket sprite. She didn't know why she imagined this. But she did. And that's not to say she disliked people. She didn't. And, increasingly, she was becoming fascinated with people. How they thought, what they said, how they behaved. It's just that she was scared by too many of them. All at once.

Jamie drifted towards the glass door of Court 1.

"It's weird, isn't it, Robbie?"

"What is?"

Why would he know what she was talking about, after all? People often said that to Jamie.

"Well, how do I know what you're thinking, Jamie?" Sometimes followed by: *"I'm nae a mind reader!"*

Oblivious, Jamie continued. "It's just weird. That in a way it's just a door. But it's glass. And you can see through it."

She'd been through glass doors before. But this was the first time she had fully understood: it was a glass door...

"Aye," Robbie replied. "You're not wrong." He smirked and raised his eyebrows, but Jamie didn't see. She was lost.

But also found.

Chapter 32
The Court – Part Three

She stood on the court. A series of small wooden planks. Intertwined. Intersecting. And white walls. White walls surrounding the stage. White walls. No memories.

Just now.

She stood on the 'T'. She remembered what the coach had said. Jamie was ready, eagle-eyed, primed to take that first shot. Then she realised she hadn't got a racket. Or even a ball. That was going to hold her back.

"You'll be needing these!"

"Aye. Thanks."

Jamie dropped the ball, lifted the racket and hit. The ball died. It was like a stone by the stream. How was this the same ball they'd been using the other day? She tried again, but with the same result. This ball's a joke, she thought. It wasn't as easy as she thought.

There was a knock at the door. Jamie heard the knock. It echoed through the blank, empty walls of the court. Who could it be? It was the night, after all. Too early for the milkman.

There was nothing, just the rain splashing onto the glass of the door. Then a face. Her heart stopped. An old man. His face long and angular. Jamie noticed his nose, which was long too, like a Roman soldier's, she thought. She seemed to see lots of people like him!

"Well! You gonna let me in or what?"

"I don't know who you are!"

"I used to play here. I play here. Here's my squash racket." He offered the racket to the glass.

Jamie paused. Then she opened the door for him.

"Thank God for that. Do you realise how wet it is outside?"

The man walked in and shook the rain off his sodden clothes. Jamie noticed that despite his advancing years, he was wearing a hoodie. He flicked it back to reveal a full head of long, straight grey hair.

"Calm down," the man said. "You look like you've seen a ghost!"

Jamie noticed he had a Scottish accent.

Robbie returned from the gym behind the squash courts and stood beside Jamie.

"Maybe we have," said Robbie.

The man looked at them both.

"What are you doing here? It's the middle of the night!"

"Well," Jamie replied, "we could say the same about you."

"I couldn't sleep. So, I thought I'd come here. I used to love it here. I loved playing squash; it suited me. Still love it now, like an old boot that feels comfortable as you try it on. Like a squash Cinderella, I can still get to the ball. If I'm on my toes. Ready. On the 'T'. You're footballers, aren't you?" the man said.

"How d'ya know we're footballers?"

"I know," the man said, gesturing with his finger, "because I'm one too!"

He went and sat down on one of the black plastic chairs on the carpeted area outside the court.

Robbie and Jamie knelt next to him.

"You don't know who I am, do you?"

They both shrugged.

"But that doesn't matter. No one likes a bragger. What matters is that we all met. On this rainy night. In the Lake District. And we're talking about squash. What were the chances?"

"Aye," Jamie laughed. "That's true."

"You ever heard of Brian Clough?"

Jamie shrugged again. "Aye, I think so."

The man turned his face to one side and stared at her.

"You think so?"

"Aye, I have!" Robbie joined in. "He was a manager."

The man turned to Robbie and looked him in the eye.

"You know about things, don't you, son? I can see that. And you can play. Football, I mean. I mean, you can really play."

Robbie looked at him. "Aye. I think so. Now I can."

"He's really good. He's with Celtic. And he's gonna play for Celtic one day," Jamie said.

"Celtic," the man went on. "I had a trial with them. They said I was too small. And I was. Back then."

The man stared into the distance, past them both, back to a previous time. Or here in a previous time.

"Where was I? Aye, Cloughie. Now, there was a man ahead of his time. Do you know what he would do with the team sometimes after training?"

Jamie was lost in his words. Robbie thought to himself, this was how he'd been with Fred, all those years before, sitting next to him in the old people's home, hearing his tales of Patsy Gallacher. He felt the carpet in the lounge under his skinny knees.

The man's eyes started to glaze, to moisten. Jamie noticed rain dripping from his long hair, which he'd swept across his forehead and back behind his ear. But there was no rain in his eyes. This was the joy of remembering something. Something special. Back then. Back now.

"Aye. He would take us to play squash. That he would. The other lads were having none of it. 'What's he thinking? I wanna go to the pub. To the races. What's with all this poncy squash rubbish?'

"You can imagine it. Yeah, maybe you can't, I don't know. Well, anyway, we're standing there in this wee squash club, we're all muddy, fresh from the training ground. Still in our strip. 'Lads', he went on, 'to have an edge, you've got to think differently. And squash players think differently. I know you would've all gone to the pub or whatever. But you're playing squash with me. Now. And let's see if any of you so-called athletes have what it takes to beat an old has-been like me.'

"And no one did of course. No one could ever beat Brian. And we didn't want to. Really. Because he was Cloughie. Anyway," he continued, suddenly standing up and taking his racket from his bag and walking towards the glass wall of the court, "are you gonna beat me or what?"

Later, after she'd drifted into a long-deserved sleep, Jamie found herself on the court again.

Dear Diary,

Well, that sleep lasted a long time! LOL. But seriously. Thing is, it's 2am! Why am I STILL awake?! I've cycled, run, and played squash. Admittedly, I didn't play for long, but I've googled it and seen it's consistently up there in the top two of all sports in terms of aerobic and anaerobic levels.

Apparently, it's not yet in the Olympics, which is strange as you'd have thought they'd have been all over it. I watched a game on YouTube earlier and it looked exhausting, like sprinting and stopping, sprinting and stopping, over and over and over. No wonder Robbie enjoyed it. He's always done stuff like that. That helped him when he was younger, when he was breaking all those bones ... that was when I first came to Clydebank. Yes, Robbie. He took to it so easily, too. OMG, he is so annoying like that!

But you'd have thought the 'people' who came up with the marathon – the ultimate test – would be into the idea of squash. That got me thinking about the original Olympics. I loved studying Ancient Greece when I was at primary school. All the competitors were naked! Yuck! I remember reading about the pankration, a combination of wrestling and boxing. The only rules were no biting or eye gouging! And all the competitors were covered in oil! Sorry for all the OMGs, but OMG!

Anyway, where was I? Yeah, actually, where was I? Sorry, Diary. I do that a lot. I must fry your brain. Well, your brain might well be fried if you were covered in oil and were competing in Ancient Greece. Obviously, that's if books were allowed to compete. And if you were real. ☹ ☹

But on a serious note, I did feel something different today. It got to the point with football, where I dreaded walking onto the pitch. It just seemed too big. Too much going on. Too much random stuff. Too many people shouting. Too loud. But when I walked onto that court today, it just seemed different. Well, at least today it did. I felt different. I just felt calmer, even though I was still doing sport.

Anyway, night night.

When I enter the court, the room becomes my world, and I'm separated from the chaos of what's outside. Through my racket, I take control of what goes on in this world, manoeuvring the ball where I want, choosing the speed of the ball and inventing ways to strike the ball, finding angles and variations that become visible only when I immerse myself into this world. My mind becomes free to discover the possibilities open to me in this separate universe. I practise alone, just me and the ball, connected only through the strings of my racket, feeling the rhythm of the bounce and the sound of the ricochet. Balance, control, movement, and smoothness fill the world.

When I play others, they try to disrupt the calm, but I take control. I resist their actions and feed off them. I harness their actions and use the ball to lead them where I want them to go. The strings of my racket control the ball, control the opponent, take control of the chaos. Not total control, but just enough.

When I have finished, maybe I can carry this with me into the chaos outside.

Maybe.

Chapter 33
The Battle

I looked up at the sky. It was beautiful. Unbelievably beautiful. Why were we here in this hell when above us, just looked so – heavenly?

I knew I should be sleeping. Grabbing something, however brief. Sleep was the one chance to escape this nightmare, at least for a while. And hopefully, I'd be dreaming of home. Of having fun at a summer fete, biking with friends, swimming in a lake. Not this.

A rat scuttled across my foot. I heard it splash into the muddy quagmire to my left. I once knew a time when I would have jumped a mile at such a thing. But those days had gone. I was numb. Dead to the world, in the dank misery of the trench, I started to sleep. At last.

The whistle went. Shrill, piercing. In contrast to my hazy vision.

Equally clear came the command.

"Come on boys, this is it! Now! Over we go!"

My eyes were now fully focused. Scanning everything around me. Robotic, mechanical motion everywhere. A flurry of activity as everyone readied themselves, engaged their rifles, and then ... then clambered the ladder into the darkness.

Into what lay ahead.

'Peep, peep', went the whistle again. How strange – the playground or factory whistle piercing the blood and thunder of this infernal war.

It was over.

I didn't have time to look up. But if I had, I'd have seen it was neither day nor night. Just a still twilight that hung above me. Observing.

I made my way forward through the sludge. The shattering machine-gun fire smashed through the darkness, exploding in my ears. Soldiers, my friends, fell down. Instantly. Gone. Still I moved on. Forward. Always forward. No time to plan, no time to think. Just do.

Then nothing. The unrelenting machine-gun fire and explosions vanished. I lay there in the sodden earth. Looking up at the stars. The stars that still looked down. Unmoved. Like the whole world had been paused. Well, my world, at least.

Boom!

I blinked.

A face looked down over me.

He bent down into the mud and picked me up. He looked at me with his steely eyes, one green and one blue.

"This isn't over. It's never over!"

Dear Diary

I can't sleep. What a dream! I feel exhausted. Think I've read too much of Mum's book! It was like I was back there in those trenches.

I have so many weird dreams. I never dream of Mum. Well, not any more. Sorry, Mum. For ages, I couldn't think of you, not even to picture your face. Your beautiful face. One more time.

I haven't spoken to you for a while. Sorry about that. Sometimes it's just too much. When I'm shaking with fear, my head pounds. You know, right here. And I just want it to stop. The thoughts. And sometimes just … I just think they never will. They never will. And maybe the sadness will always be there. And it's just too much. I wish you were here so you could hold me. One more time. One last time. Like you used to. You were so kind.

I don't know how I'd cope without Robbie. Maybe that's what the dream was. Anyway, it was bloody scary. It must have been horrendous. Those poor men. But Amy sounds amazing. Like a beacon of hope. Just by being Amy. Just by being there. Listening.

But Mum. Mum, I'm so glad you wrote about Amy. Introduced me to her world. And maybe your world, too. Thank you, Mum. I love you, Mum.

I'm sorry I can't write any more. God, I was ok when I was walking with Robbie. Why is it so quick? Out of the blue.

Again. One more time.

Chapter 34
The Lake

Jamie went to the train station with Robbie. The sky was overcast and the clouds looked brimful of damp sadness, ready to be squeezed out at any time. Jamie felt numb. Not really present.

Robbie coming to stay with her in the Lakes had certainly picked her up, to say the least! She had been crumbling, bit by bit, day by day. But she knew that Robbie had to get back for his Celtic training, and he had some big games coming up. And she knew that however comfortable she felt around Robbie, however strong she felt when he was near her, she had to find the strength now to run that final leg by herself. He would still be there, of course. He would always be there. He would always be there, to always be 'truth'. But she also had to find her own truth.

"I'll see you when you get back. Take care, Jamie. Remember, keep looking forward."

Jamie nodded.

Keep looking forward.

And with that, Robbie Blair had gone.

With his strength and positivity coursing through her veins, Jamie had only one idea in her mind. Go for a run.

She even felt brave enough to take her auntie's dog, Buddy. He seemed keen! They breezed past the holidaymakers, taking in their holiday smiles. She thought at one point that she might have knocked someone off the pavement. But then she remembered what the therapist had said and she resisted the urge to look back.

They are just thoughts, Jamie. Just thoughts. Let them fly in. And let them fly out again.

Her eyes were fixed on the distant, craggy backdrop to the town. It was inviting her onward, over the bridge, over the stile and then to where the path became more rugged, strewn with boulders and rocks.

She was keen and alert but still intent on looking forward. As she approached the summit, she ran past the grassy verge where she had met her painter friend.

Nothing's perfect, Jamie. Look around you. Nothing's perfect.

Jamie stood near the edge of the peak and took in the majestic sky spread out in front of her. She was lost in its beauty. But then, then she looked down. The massive drop beneath her suddenly unnerved her. She felt sick, giddy, the familiar quickening of her heart. She felt herself swaying. Or was that just in her mind? A thought flew into her head.

Jump!

Jump!

Jamie looked down again. But then, as quickly as the other feeling had taken over her body, she felt a sense of calm.

"Now why would I do that?" she shouted out loud to herself. And she laughed. Because it was ridiculous. It WAS laughable.

Why would you do that?

I quite like talking to myself, Jamie decided. I can give those thoughts what for!

With her new sense of purpose and resolve, she made her way down the slope, through a small coppice of trees and gazed down towards the lake. She had planned to run back once she had reached the summit, but had suddenly become entranced by the lake.

She ran down the lush downward path, hopping over the many boulders that peppered the grass. Again. Eyes only looking forward.

And then. She was there.

She hadn't really prepared for the lake, for water. Well, she hadn't prepared for it at all. She had no swimming costume. But she was in shorts, so a paddle would do. She took her trainers and socks off and put them neatly by a large mossy rock. She then moved away from the flat, sculpted stone that encircled this side of the lake and dipped her foot in. The glacial chill sent a shudder through her body. As she gingerly placed her other foot in, a curious thing happened above her. Seemingly, out of nowhere, the clear blue sky was joined by a group of dark, foreboding clouds. Like the painter said, even on the clearest, sunniest day, you may only be moments away from a dark cloud on the horizon.

And with that, the rain began to fall. But the rain felt good. Buddy was off doing his thing, lost in his own playful adventures. The cool droplets on her flesh, combined with the icy ripples on her toes, made her feel alive. Totally in the now.

Onward, Jamie continued through the waters. A swan came into view, observing her. She was now thigh-deep. Her legs had become used to the temperature now, but it was still undeniably cold. The rain continued to fall, and Jamie looked at the concentric circles the droplets made as they struck the surface. And then, as she continued to gaze into the lake, she remembered. It came to her in a flash.

Reflected in the water, she could see the mean face of Bruce, the football coach. Glaring back at her.

"Take a long, hard look at yourself in the mirror, Jamie! A long, hard look!"

And with that, the face was gone. Jamie closed her eyes. Maybe it was her fault. All of it. Losing those games. The Cup Final. The broken leg.

Losing Mum.

Maybe it was all her fault. She was a curse. On everyone.

They are just thoughts, Jamie. Just thoughts, the painter called out across the lake.

Jamie opened her eyes. It was still raining. A roll of thunder echoed across the landscape. But then, in the distance, arching the rocky peaks, a beautiful rainbow appeared, vibrant yet soft in the clear light.

And as the thunder rolled in the distance, as Bruce's words echoed in her mind, she stared down into the lake and looked.

Looked for Jamie.

And there she was, staring back. Like a flickering cine film image on the rippling screen of the lake. But she didn't stare into her reflection. She looked. Really looked. Had she ever looked at herself like this before? This deeply?

And what did she see?

She was a good person. Who did good things. And who tried her best. That is what she saw.

That is what she saw.

And, fuelled by the warmth of this thought, Jamie dived into the lake. All other thoughts that may have been hiding in her mind, ready to pounce, were swept away as she surged through the waters.

At one with the lake.

Dear Mum

I'm exhausted. But I will get there, Mum.

I will do it.

I know I won't always feel like this...

But this has got to be good, hasn't it, Mum?

Chapter 35
The Teacher

Whilst having breakfast with Auntie Jackie, the subject of what Jamie was going to get up to for the last week of the Easter holidays came up.

"So, what are you thinking, Jamie? I'm at work again all week. Do you want me to see if there's some kind of football training going on?"

Jamie smiled weakly. She could think of nothing worse. She wasn't ready for football, even back in Clydebank, where she knew people. But football here, where she knew no one? Strangers all looking at her, judging her? While she sat there panicking, something hit the switch. The thoughts came flooding back. An onslaught. No.

"Hmm ... maybe not," she replied.

"Well, ok. But you need to do something." Her auntie paused. "It would be good for you."

What do you mean, 'good for you'? Jamie thought. Who had she been talking to? She could guess.

Her auntie continued. "Listen, Jamie, a friend of mine's a teacher at a local secondary school, and I know they're putting on some music and drama classes and clubs this week. Is that something that could interest you?"

It could.

It should.

Jamie's initial thought, her initial response, was the same as always: her heart raced, her pulse quickened. Her breathing became shallow, from her chest, or maybe higher. Her face showed everything. She couldn't lie. Her face and her feelings were very close. Like best mates. Especially her eyes. If she felt something – good, bad, or ugly – you could bet all the money in the world that it would tell in her eyes.

She felt all the above. Obviously. But she saw the woman she had been reading about in her mind. Amy. What would Amy do? So, she said this instead: "Well. Ok."

And ok is always a good enough start.

They pulled into the sparse car park at Lakelands Academy. The empty parking bays escalated in Jamie's mind. The parking spaces, those empty parking spaces, seemed to go on forever. Would the car park ever end?

When would it end?

Jamie walked into the school hall. School halls—did they all look the same? She was warmed by the structure, the roof, the generous space meandering in and out beneath her footsteps.

There was a man stood by a table with a sign saying: Music Club. He was a cool-looking, older dude with short, greying dreads.

Jamie went over to the table, gave a little shrug and made some sort of sound.

"Hi! How are you? Are you ready to make some music?"

Jamie paused. Her heart raced. The same old. But she liked him. There was something in his eyes. You could tell in his eyes. After all.

After all.

In the end, just two teenagers –Jamie and another girl – were taken up the stairs to the music department of Lakelands Academy. They both looked lost.

The other girl had long dark hair. She was called Emily. Her eyes sparkled. But then they didn't. Suddenly. And Jamie could see that. Like Robbie could. Empty.

The man with the greying dreads began.

"Right then. Nice to meet you both. Thanks for coming to my club. This week, we are going to be learning all about music, about being in a band. What it feels like to play an instrument, to make music, to play in a band. To be part of a band."

Jamie hadn't thought of herself as musical before. Not until now.

"So, we're going to start with the drums."

Jamie looked around the room. There were three drum kits set up, four if you included the teacher's.

"Right," he said, "let's start!"

The man kicked the bass drum. Bang! "Right, do the same."

Both girls kicked the bass drum.

Next, he hit the smaller, upright drum. It had a tight skin and made a higher, raspier sound. The girls hit the snare.

The man continued. "Right, hit the bass drum and then the snare. Bass, snare. Like this."

The man demonstrated with his drum kit, speaking as he played.

"Boom   chaaa.   Boom   chaaa.   Boom   chaaa. 1...2...1...2...1...2...1...2..."

Jamie looked at the man. Closely. She looked at his foot. She looked at his hand. Boom chaaa. Boom chaaa. She tried it.

"Nice," he said, smiling. "Keep it going. Boom chaaa. Boom chaaa. Like a Roman soldier. Marching. Boom chaaa."

Boom chaaa. Boom chaaa. Jamie kicked the bass drum. She kicked it again. Boom. She felt it resonate through her body. Through her heart. Through her soul. Boom. Then the snare. The chaaa. Boom chaaa. Not only was she alive, she was alive and she could see things. She could see. Beyond herself.

Next.

"Well done, both of you. You've both done really well. You both have excellent rhythm and you can play in time. Boom chaaa. That's level 1 cracked!"

The man continued.

"So, next, we have level 2. This is the big one. It's so big that calling it level 2 doesn't do it justice. Because when you've cracked this level, not only have you made it to level 2, you've made it to a whole new world. And that is more than a new level."

Jamie sat on her drum stool, ready. Ready for the next world.

Both girls looked at him.

"So, we've got boom chaaa, boom chaaa..." He demonstrated. The girls followed him.

"Now. This is the thing."

He pointed to two cymbals that lay on top of each other, one concave and one convex. Ready to meet. The cymbals were mounted on a metal pole and underpinning the whole system was a pedal. When Jamie pressed the pedal, the cymbal, or the hi-hat as it was called, made a muted, controlled 'ching'. When she took her foot off the pedal, the hi-hat made a loud, unbridled scream. Jamie preferred the muted sound.

The man hit the hi-hat – 1...2...3...4. "Just do that. Foot down."

Jamie and Emily repeated what the man was demonstrating. They repeated it exactly.

"Now," he continued, "boom chaaa. Boom chaaa. Boom chaaa ... NOW!"

And with that, he started hitting the hi-hat with his right hand. Ching ching ching ching...

Jamie tried it. Like the man said. Boom chaaa. Boom chaaa. Steady. Perfect. Then repeat. Every time.

Then. She was ready. She hit the hi-hat. After two beats, it all broke down. Her bass drum started following the snare. It was tantalisingly close. She could feel it. But every time she tried it, it broke down.

The man smiled.

"Everyone's the same, Jamie. We are all the same. If it was that easy, then everyone would play the drums. It's tricky. Life is tricky. Life is complicated. Go again, Jamie. You've got this."

Jamie took a deep breath. She really had got this. Come on. She kicked the bass drum. Boom! She hit the snare. Chaaa! Repeat. Repeat. Repeat. Now! Ching ching ching. Jamie hit the hi-hat. It was as if her brain had been split in two. One half was able to do the boom chaaa and the other the ching ching ching. The heartbeat, the vision. Now she was feeling it too.

Feeling the world around her. What would Amy think?

Chapter 36
How Do You Know?

Late one night, Jamie and Auntie Jackie were playing cards. She had taught Jamie how to play a variety of games and Jamie enjoyed them all. She looked forward to the comforting routine of playing and was disappointed when anything got in the way of that.

As they were coming to the end of a game, her auntie started talking to her, more like a conversation rather than anything about cards.

"Have you enjoyed yourself, Jamie? I know I've been at the hospital a lot and left you to your own devices ... but hopefully, you've enjoyed yourself. Hopefully, it's been good for you."

The fire crackled. Jamie felt the glow on her face. She looked all around the busy walls of her auntie's lounge – the shelves stacked with books of all descriptions, the random lampshades, and the obscure paintings. They all meant something to her auntie, but, in a way, even after just two weeks, this randomness, and the uniformity of her room, had begun to mean something to Jamie too. In a way, she thought it was weird. Because in other respects, she didn't like 'too much'. She struggled with football for that reason. There were too many things going on, too many people speaking, shouting, thinking. But this seemed to be ok, and it even seemed to help her. For some reason.

"It's been great, Auntie Jackie," Jamie replied. "And dunnae worry about deserting me. I've loved it here in the Lakes. It's been great." Jamie smiled faintly, but it looked more than that to her auntie. And it felt more than that to Jamie.

They finished the game and put the cards on the table.

Her auntie pulled up her knees to her chin on the big, creased leather chair.

"So, what are you doing tomorrow? Your last day."

Jamie didn't like the way she said 'your last day'. She stopped smiling, but this time, no one could see the change in her mood. It was too quick. Probably. She didn't even like it when people said 'first day'. Too much pressure. Like a school trip. Or a first day at school. What could go wrong? What would go wrong? What had gone wrong?

Jamie liked 'in-between'.

"I don't know, really. I was thinking of going for one last run. Maybe calling in at the squash club and saying goodbye."

Her auntie looked amazed. "The squash club! Since when have you been there?"

"Oh, me and Robbie. We went a few times. Brookside. I really like it."

Her auntie looked at her. "Jamie, you're a strange one. But we do love you. Your mum would be very proud. She was a strange one, too. Bless her."

The next morning, Jamie woke up instantly to warm sunlight beaming through the slight gaps in the curtains and onto her face. She felt good. She felt refreshed after a good night's sleep and her mind, for now, felt free of any negative thoughts. Get up, shower, run. A simple enough plan.

And when she turned off the tap after brushing her teeth, she actually felt it turn off. She knew she had turned it off. And she didn't check. She knew it wasn't going to carry on filling the sink and eventually engulf the floor and bring a sodden, saturated, plastered ceiling down in crashing apocalyptic episodes. Even though these thoughts flashed in her mind, she knew. She had turned the tap off. She was pretty sure, to be honest. And that seemed to be enough. For now.

Jamie took her usual path up the street, over the bridge, turned left by the stile and then made steady progress through the gradually more challenging terrain of her favourite hill. She made her normal shortcut through the small coppice and back onto the stony path and then she saw him. She saw his head at first and his beard, just above the rocky outcrop in front of him. She ran towards him and then started walking, cushioned by the grass, but still conscious not to disturb him. The painter continued to gaze into the blue sky, lost in its unfathomable beauty.

"How are you, Jamie?" he asked, without looking around.

"Good," Jamie said. "Real good. I turned the tap off today without checking once. And I ran here without looking back once. Just looking forward. I kind of made myself just look forward, but kind of didn't need to either. Kind of."

The man turned around. His face, Jamie thought, as always, looked a bit like a Roman's, with his angular features, his long nose and his neat beard and moustache. She often felt like that. She could see someone and instantly decide what face their century belonged in. Like instantly.

"Tudor!" she had said, on first meeting one of Robbie's friends from the Celtic youth team.

"No, I'm Connor!" he'd answered, awkwardly.

Robbie had laughed, albeit not visibly.

"Medieval!" she had called out, on meeting her new supply maths teacher.

The teacher didn't take to that too well and promptly gave Jamie a detention. But Jamie knew what she meant.

Seriously!

The artist smiled. A warm, genuine smile that lifted her. She felt it. Just a smile. That's all.

"And how have you been generally?"

Jamie wasn't quite so sure. Her mind became muddled. What do I say? Generally. How have I generally been? Generally. I don't know. Bad, sometimes. Ok, sometimes. Can't get out of bed, sometimes. Played squash. Laughed. Smiled. Learnt something. Forgot something. I dunno ... what are the options?

"Hmm, good, I think. You know, pretty good."

The painter looked at her. He smiled a 'bless you' smile, as if he knew what she was saying.

Really knew.

He put his paintbrush down and continued. "The thing is, Jamie ... and I know we've talked about this before ... but nothing is perfect. Nothing is perfect. You play football, don't you?"

"Aye. I used to."

He brought his hands together. Clasped. She liked it. There was intent. He knew what he was going to say.

"Well, let's imagine a game. I used to like football too, Jamie. Imagine a game where it's raining the whole time. It's a bleak, rainy game. What do you say in Scotland? Dreich?"

"Aye, dreich."

She knew 'dreich' all right. Jamie nodded.

The man went on.

"And you've done absolutely nothing in the game whatsoever."

Jamie imagined that. Scrub that, she remembered that. All too familiar.

"But then, out of nowhere, out of the darkness, you score. Your team wins. Is the whole of that game, as a memory, complete, unbridled happiness? Or is it another all-encompassing, unreachable cloud of misery? Or is it, maybe, a bit of both?"

"Maybe."

He used that word a lot. Considering he seemed so sure.

The man continued, staring not at Jamie this time, but at the sky. Again.

Jamie, with her 'Tudor!' head on, felt her conversation – her time – with the painter was drawing to an end.

She listened.

"Maybe. Even when you've felt low. At your lowest..."

Jamie's face rocked gently to the movement of the painter's words.

"Even at those times when you've felt so low that you've felt..."

Jamie felt there were people's faces flashing over the sky.

The painter turned away.

"Just know that, even in the bleakest moments, on that pitch, some-times you felt ok. There really *were* moments of sunshine. In fact, there were lots of them. You just can't remember them now."

Jamie understood. She looked at the painter.

But the painter had gone.

Chapter 37
The Manager

When the girls knew Jamie was back, they immediately asked Bruce to put her back in the team. Jamie wasn't sure of his actual response, but she was added to the WhatsApp group again, and she was put in the side for the next game.

Towards the end of that game, they were all yearning for the final whistle. But, though it loomed, it just would not come. They were still kind of trying, but the spark had gone. That vital spark, that invisible spirit that normally galvanised the girls in big moments of the game. And the more Bruce shouted – no, ranted – the less effect his anger had. It was never the most effective weapon in his managerial toolbox – it just had the opposite effect on most of the girls (probably on all of the girls) – but on this day, it had an even more negative influence. The girls were like lost sprites, ashen-faced, hollow-eyed and devoid of any spirit at all.

Apart from that, they've still got every chance, Robbie Blair chuckled to himself from the sideline. He was in his Celtic Youth team kit, but wearing a black hoodie over the top. He was a strong-looking boy of medium height for his age, and his crown of tousled curls blew around his face in the fresh breeze. Robbie watched on.

At last, the whistle sounded. The girls trudged off the muddy grass and onto the side of the pitch. They grabbed their water bottles and some of the girls snatched up their navy-blue team hoodies.

Most of them looked down, or glanced awkwardly in Bruce's general direction, without really catching his eye. Jamie felt stronger now than she used to. And she looked him in the eye.

"So, are ye pleased with yeselves?" he bellowed in his gravelly burr. His unshaven, broad chin jutted towards them. To Jamie.

"Are ya?"

Jamie thought, wait, was this a rhetorical question? Like they did in English? She thought for a moment about replying but then decided against it. Maybe it was then.

Who would be first into the lions' den. It was too tense for question marks.

Jamie still looked on defiantly. But the answer did not come from Jamie Campbell. The answer came from the most unlikely of sources. Little Lyla McTavish.

"It's gone," she said.

"It's gone, ye say! Ha!" Bruce boomed back, smiling in a way, but even more annoyed in another.

"Aye, it's gone."

"Well then, if you're such an expert, wee Lyla, would you care to expand on your insights into the game by sharing with us what exactly it is that has gone?"

This was definitely not a rhetorical question, thought Jamie. He definitely wants an answer.

Meanwhile, Robbie looked on. Tapping a ball between his feet. He looked casual and uninterested to an observer, but he was taking in every word.

The atmosphere was tense. If you had an aversion to confrontation, then this was not the place to be. Anywhere but here. Jamie would normally have used her imagination to take herself away to a remote

Scottish hideaway, where she'd tip her toes in the tranquil, lapping waters of a beguiling loch. But today, now, she was rooted, anchored in the claggy turf of the home pitch. Braced for whatever was to come. Progress.

As little Lyla stepped towards Bruce, Jamie thought she was like Oliver Twist, daring to ask for another bowl of Ready Brek or whatever they ate back then.

But instead of 'MORE!', her key message was 'GONE!!!!!!!!!!!!!!!!!!!!!'

"Well. It just seems that the spirit has gone. The team spirit. It is nae there."

She had been very brave. No one else had dared to stick their head above the parapet and say anything. But as her words faded into the chilly air, she gave a little shrug, an apologetic grimace.

"Well, is that reet, little lady?! And yer an expert now in sports psychology?!"

"No. I'm nae expert. But I know when something has gone."

If this was one of those funny cartoon films, this would be the point when the meek little penguin turns to the thousands of ungalvanised 'watching on' penguins and bellows:

"Am I REEEEEEEEEEEEEEEEEEEEEEEEEEEEEETTTTTTTTTT-TTTTTTTTTTTTT?"

This would then result in a tidal wave of cheer and euphoric defiance from the regalvanised penguin masses.

But this was not the South Pole, and Lyla McTavish was not a penguin. And this was not a film.

So, no one said anything. Lyla retreated to the shadows. The girls continued to stand in awkward silence. For a while. Until, eventually, a different voice broke the silence.

Now that Jamie had her spirit back, she knew when the team's spirit had gone.

"But she's right. It has gone. And if we're honest–"

"Who are WE?"

"Then, well, it's been missing for a while."

There were still no mumblings from the chorus of penguins, but this was a development.

Bruce took a sharp intake of breath. Dramatically. And he twisted his head to the left, pursing his lips.

"Is that reet?"

"Aye," Jamie said. "Aye, it is."

Bruce twisted his head to the right and pulled in another breath through his nose. He was thinking, but maybe he had already made up his mind.

"Aye, well then, maybe I'm gone too," he said softly. The rant and the sarcasm had now dissipated into something more resigned, more human.

And with that, he was gone. Trudging across the neighbouring pitches to the car park. Not an angry figure now. Just a lonely, sad one.

The girls looked at each other, aware of the gravity of the situation. What were they feeling? Losing the game was now irrelevant. It had been deleted. And what of this sudden departure? How did they feel? Some of them might have wished for it anyway. But it was weird – maybe sad, or saddish – that Bruce had gone. He'd been with them for a while now. But the shouting had got worse. For whatever reason. And the shouting always made things worse. Jamie knew.

"Well, that was awkward!" Isla said.

The girls laughed. Isla always made the girls laugh. Especially at times like these.

"But," Jamie continued, "what are we going to do now? We're halfway through the season. And we've got nae manager."

Then. Out of the blue. Came a voice.

"I'll be your manager."

It was Robbie. Robbie Blair.

Chapter 38
What Do You Remember?

It was a Saturday afternoon. Robbie had been to training at the Celtic Youth training ground. His white shorts were muddy and his unruly curls flowed out from the side of his hoodie.

Jamie's dad answered the door. He looked preoccupied, Robbie thought. But then again, he always looked like that.

"Morning, Robbie," he said.

Jamie's dad liked Robbie. He was solid. Reliable. Good for Jamie. He had been a constant presence in Jamie's life, ever since they'd moved to Clydebank. Ever since...

"She's around somewhere."

"Aye. She's always around somewhere." Robbie grinned.

Her dad was just about to shout out her name when she appeared, her football socks half-mast. She was wearing shorts and a hoodie. Like Robbie, locks of hair cascaded from her hood, tracing the side of her pale face.

"Where you going?" he asked, peering over his spectacles and grasping a bundle of folders that seemed intent on slipping away from his grasp.

Jamie didn't know. She hadn't even thought about it. Just leaving her bedroom. Out of the house. Into the world. Wasn't that enough? In a way, it was...

Robbie didn't know either, but his 'didn't know' sounded more measured, more planned. As if he *did* know, but just hadn't realised it yet. If that was possible.

"Well, have fun."

Jamie's dad was just glad she was out.

At Glasgow Central Station, they looked at the giant board with all the destinations and departures and arrivals.

"I know," Robbie suddenly announced. "Saltcoats. Let's go there. It's been a while. Saltcoats was important for me. It helped me. It was the first time I could run after my last broken leg. Cushioned by the sand and the sea, I really started to believe. Maybe it could help you, too."

Jamie shrugged. "Sure. Why not."

And so they hopped on the train that was bound for Saltcoats. To the seaside.

There was nobody on the train. Nobody at all. It was like they were the last people alive. Well, apart from the train driver, presumably. They could sit where they wanted. Anywhere. Jamie didn't always like that. A blank canvas. Too much choice. Too much room to think. But she was with Robbie, so she was more 'sure'. They sat down on either side of one of the tables. When the train got going, Jamie could see that Robbie was looking quizzical. He was squinting, looking ready to speak.

"So, this OCD thing."

"Aye, this thing."

"Well, what is it exactly? I mean, I get that you think you cannae remember whether you switched the oven off. I think I've had that. I think. Or if you've locked a door. But is it more than that? How come we didn't see you for about a month?"

Jamie gulped and thought. Long and hard. It was one of those times when she felt she had too much to say but couldn't think of how to express it.

She gulped again and looked out of the window at the conveyor belt of back gardens drifting past amidst the rhythmic, pulsing traction of the train. Filling her mind with other people's worlds.

"I just think the worst things all the time. And I think I've actually said them. Done them. If I've handed an essay in, I'll ask for it back 'cos I think I've scrawled swearwords all over it, called Mr McNeil a xxxx."

"But you know you haven't really? Surely?"

Surely? I'm not sure of anything?

Even that statement was a question.

Jamie looked at Robbie. Long and hard. Like he did her.

"I don't know anything. I feel like my mind is like a chariot, and once a thought enters my mind, no matter what it is, instantly the whip is cracked and the horses bolt. Immediately, I'm lost, galloping away. Anything is possible. And I did it all. Yes, Boss. It was me. I did it. Whatever it was."

Robbie was trying his best. He really was. They were all trying their best.

"Did what? What did you do?"

Jamie closed her eyes and jutted her jaw. She averted his gaze.

"I don't know. I know that when me and Dad have been driving, and there's a bump, I just think we've knocked someone over. Ended their life. That's what I think. I check the road. I check it endlessly. I stare at the grass verge, until there's nothing left to see. Then I just fill in the gaps with the worst thoughts."

As soon as they arrived at Saltcoats, they made for the beach and started running.

Her toes sank into the wet sand.

The sky was blue, but the wind unravelled as she ran, skipping and clipping the waves as they reached the end of their journey, anchored by the wet sand.

Robbie ran too. He was barefoot. His curly locks joined forces with the wind and breezed into Jamie's view.

He turned around to her.

"But you must know whether you've done something or not? Do you not know that? You know you're here. Now. Don't ya?"

Jamie thought. For a moment. For a while. For her life.

Did she know that?

On the slow, winding way back to Glasgow, Jamie again gazed out through the train window.

She looked at Robbie.

"If I'm down, if you told me something, anything, I'd believe it. I'd believe I'd done it."

Robbie looked back at Jamie.

"But you do. You do remember stuff. What's your name?"

"Jamie!"

"There you go. You can do it."

"Thanks!" Jamie clapped sarcastically, like a seal.

Robbie continued. "What did you do earlier? At 12:05?"

Jamie looked at him, alarmed but clear in her mind. For a change.

"I got on a train. With you."

Robbie looked at her back.

Because sometimes that's all you need to do.

Chapter 39
Mountain IV

They were getting nearer now. Nothing was said, but they both knew it. Felt it. They'd ascended all the steep rocky slopes.

All but the brightest of colours had painted Jamie's views until now, and she had been waiting for the clearest of colours to come.

"Look!" Robbie said. "Water!"

Lush green grass lay before them, and then this blaze of green led to the most serene loch that Jamie had ever seen. Even in her dreams. The clear crystalline water stretched out before them, inviting and beguiling. The sunlight twinkled.

Jamie, caught up in the loch's hypnotic gaze, walked towards it. Dipping her toes in the icy waters, she felt she had come home. Again. She walked in deeper and deeper, without a thought or a pause. She jumped in, as before, embracing its glacial clarity.

And then it happened. Again. Everything. All at once. The juggernaut had stopped. The chariot was no longer careering out of control in a thousand directions. Just one, clear, distilled thought.

I am good!

Dear Diary

So, we've broken up for the summer holidays. I was so looking forward to summer.

I was on the crest of a wave, if you like. OMG, that's rubbish, even for a diary entry! I felt it in my brain. A glow. I know I get it sometimes.

Now it feels like no times.

Did it ever exist?

When Robbie took over the team and I was playing better, stronger, with more confidence, I was gliding past people who I'd felt worried about for a while. But not now. Some people say it's in my head. They don't know it, but they're right.

Why is everything different, only a few days later, maybe even just one day? I've lost count. I hate weeks. I just like days. Or maybe hours. Or even minutes. I can't go any less than that, can I? Otherwise, what's the point? What's the point in seconds? Moments? What's the point in them if they don't all add up in a neat line, you know, of life, of happiness? Moments aren't enough. I can't remember moments. I JUST REMEMBER WEEKS. Weeks turn into months, and I HATE THEM EVEN MORE.

PS I couldn't sleep, so here's some other news: I had a WhatsApp message from Isla. She wants to form a band. She wants ME to play drums. Well, I'll think about it. I didn't realise I'd told her I play the drums. To be honest, I think I'd forgotten. ☹

Anyway, nighty night.

Chapter 40
The Race

It was Friday. Jamie was sitting in the crowded cafeteria of Saint Peter's High School. She was looking dreamily into the distance, her loaded fork making twirling motions in the air.

"What you doing Saturday?" Jamie asked.

"Got a game," Robbie replied starkly.

"Ok. Who against?"

"Hibs."

"Cool. Nice. D'ya think you'll score?"

"Aye."

That's what Jamie liked about Robbie. Robbie Blair. He was so sure. He just knew.

Just knew.

He didn't panic. Or second guess. Or worry. She knew all this, of course. He'd always been the same. Well, for as long as she'd known him. That was Robbie. Sometimes, she even thought, and she had told her therapist this, that she could 'catch it off him' – his 'sureness' about things. Was that possible? Maybe if she spent enough time with him, stood next to him, it might happen.

What if she spoke like him? Used the words he used? Reacted to things like he did? What if it was like a script? And if she did all of these things, thought all of these things, then perhaps after a while, it would become less like a script and more ... more real. She would become like him. And then she wouldn't worry about anything. Because he didn't. Or he didn't seem to anyway.

She knew deep down that wasn't possible. To become someone else. Her therapist agreed. But maybe there was something to be learned from observing how other people react and respond, and how they think. You didn't need to 'become' them, but just be inspired by their words, their thoughts. You just needed to head in that general direction. Sometimes. Maybe that was possible. Maybe.

"I think I might do that Park Run. You've done it, haven't you?" she asked, her eyes looking clearer, suddenly more focused.

"Aye, I have. I used to do the junior one. I won it. I think. Then I did the adult one. Once, I think. It's good."

"Any tips?"

Robbie looked at her. "I just run."

Jamie smiled. Classic Robbie Blair. Just run.

Jamie took the train to Glasgow Central and then caught a train to Drumchapel. She made the short walk to the course. She'd googled where it was and the route so that she could visualise it. Five kilometres. She'd done plenty of runs of this distance, but she didn't always know how far she'd gone. A bit like Robbie, she just ran.

She was surprised by how picturesque it all looked. She really was in the countryside here, she thought to herself.

She had arrived quite early. To be sure of being on time. She felt quite calm, in a good place. The birds were singing and the sky was clear and blue. There was no wind and there was a pleasing warmth in the air. Minute by minute, the lane began to fill up. It was all very organised. Lots of tracksuited people who had all been given a job, a role. Lots of the runners were wearing club running vests, and they certainly looked like proper runners. Tall and slim, they just looked like experienced runners.

It suddenly occurred to Jamie that she didn't really know how to run a race. How did you do it? Start off fast and then see how long you can keep that up? Or start off slow and then see if you can pick things up after the halfway stage? Or did you just go nice and steady for the whole thing? She really didn't have a clue. She looked around.

Maybe the answers *were all around her*. In people. And there were lots of those. Right now.

Maybe just find someone who looks like they might run pretty quickly, but not like quick as in winning the thing, but quick as in, you know, quick. Maybe then once you've identified this epic benchmark, well, then, you just run with them. Keep them next to you, run with them. In their slipstream. How hard could that be?

Well, it was a plan. It was something. She scanned all the people. Hopefully, not in a scary way. That would just be weird, after all, mentally frisking them, systematically, in a logical clockwise direction. But she scanned them all the same.

And then she saw. That was the one. He was tall and slim. Well, that wasn't a surprise – good runners normally are, aren't they? He had a club vest on, but he wasn't one of the group hovering near the front. But he looked quick.

"Excuse me, mister. Can I ask you a question?" Jamie asked. Out of the blue. She didn't even know that she was going to ask him anything. She just did.

Just did.

He looked down at her. He was tall after all. His hair was short around the back and sides, so short that you could see the skin, and on top, it was thick and slightly wavy. He had clean-cut features and Jamie thought he looked like one of the stricken soldiers arriving at Craiglockhart. He looked organised but nice as well.

She was still getting told off in English for saying something or somebody was 'nice'.

"Yuck, Jamie! Enough of nice! Push yourself."

But, what's wrong with being nice? Jamie thought. Nice. And, of course, there was nothing at all wrong with it.

"Aye. Crack on," the runner said.

Jamie went on. With no idea what she was going to say.

"Have you ever won this race?"

He smiled. "Aye."

So he was that quick, Jamie thought. Perhaps it would be pushing it to stay with him for the whole race. But you never know.

"What do you think about when you're running? What's in your head?" she asked.

"In my head? Nothing, really. I'm just trying to focus."

"But what on?"

"Just putting into practice all my training, all the runs. Everything that has led to this moment. Just trying to be free."

"Free..." Jamie repeated dreamily.

"Aye. Free." The man smiled.

"Can I be free?" Jamie asked.

The man stopped his stretching, and looked more intently at her.

"Aye," he said. "Of course you can."

Jamie smiled and thanked him. She felt calm. Even though the race was about to start.

The runners were all called to order. It was going to start in one minute. There were hundreds of people now. There was an energy in the air.

Before he left to go to the front of the assembled runners, the man said one more thing to Jamie.

"You see this watch?"

"Yeah," she replied.

"It's a great watch. It does everything. There's nothing this watch doesn't do or tell me. But during the race, I don't look at it once. Not once. Do you know what I use for a watch?"

"No," Jamie replied, almost hypnotised. For once.

The man touched his heart.

"This one," he said. "That's the only watch I use. I listen to what it says and run accordingly. Good luck."

And with that, the man wove his way to the front of the line. Where he would stay. For the whole race.

Chapter 41
Amy's Last Game – Early 1916

Once the First World War had finally finished, women's football would be banned.

And this memorable match between Fairfield Ladies and Dick Kerr Ladies would be the last time that Amy MacGregor ever played in a competitive game of football before taking up her career as a nurse.

***

Jock stood in the centre circle, his arms folded and his mind focused. There was a quiet hush in the air. The women stood around him, looking pensive.

"Right. Two things, girls. We play on Saturday. Dick Kerr Ladies. Celtic Park." He was a man of few words and, as usual, he cut straight to the chase.

"Celtic Park!" Amy gasped.

The rest of the women all looked impressed, but Amy found it hard to contain herself.

"Aye. Celtic Park, Paradise!" replied Jock. "Now, let's get to work. So that we can knock them off their perch."

Dick Kerr Ladies were a big deal in women's football. They were becoming a big deal in all football, really. Since their formation during the war, they had fast become a footballing sensation to rival even their male counterparts. They attracted crowds of up to fifty thousand. It was expected that this long-awaited clash between the rising Scottish stars, Fairfield Ladies, and their glamorous rivals from over the border would raise a similar turnout. The secret weapon in the English side was deemed to be the mighty Lily Parr. Amy had heard that she was a force to be reckoned with. Lily Parr was five feet ten inches tall, and she could strike the ball so hard that she had reputedly broken the arm of a male goalkeeper with one of her ferocious penalty strikes!

Amy was looking forward to the game. This was what she had been waiting for.

Amy and the team were working at the factory on the day of the game. She didn't see this as unfortunate; it was just the way it was. The war was still going on and bullets, unfortunately, still needed to be made. More than ever. Sadly. When the whistle pierced through the factory walls, signalling the end of their shift at 1pm, she began to think about the game.

At last.

She unpacked the brown paper parcel that contained her sandwiches and sat on the main steps into the factory. Jock saw Amy and came over to talk to her.

"How are you getting to the game, Amy? Me and the girls are going to take the tram. Are ya in?"

Amy thought. This was the biggest game of her life. She needed time to think. To focus. And something inside her knew that there was somehow more to this game. The war had, sadly, dragged on, way past the initial, breezy predictions that it would 'be over by Christmas'. It just kept slowly grinding on, taking more innocent souls in its path, every single day.

"No, Jock. Thanks, I'll walk. I need time to think. To prepare. And to feel."

"No problem, Amy. We'll see you there."

Jock winked at Amy. He understood her. He knew how she worked. Knew to give her space.

When Amy was in sight of Celtic Park, she suddenly realised that she was no longer alone. How had she not seen them?! What had started as a trickling stream had now evolved into a flowing river of caps and pipes sweeping her up, engulfing her.

Where was this leading?

As the teeming throng of fans approached the entrance to Celtic Park, she meandered away from them towards the players' entrance.

A boy, probably about fourteen, stepped out from the crowd.

"Good luck, Amy!" he shouted. There was a glimmer in his eye. He knew.

When Amy walked out onto the pitch, she felt the roar of the crowd fill her soul. She soaked it up, determined to enjoy each last moment, until it was spent.

Dick Kerr Ladies impressed Amy. They were deserving of their reputation. They were a strong, physical side and they went one nil up with a powerhouse thirty-yard shot from Lily Parr that almost broke the net.

"Bloody 'ell!" a burly man behind the goal shouted. "Are ya sure that's not James McGrory playing?"

Fairfield Ladies went two down just before halftime with another goal from Parr, this time from the penalty spot. This time, no bones were broken. Amy had had a quiet game. A few nice touches, but nothing had really happened for her. Nothing had really happened for the whole team.

A man looked down at her from the terraces. He had a snarling face.

"Get back to the kitchen, darling. Y'ar no match for these!"

Amy stopped in her tracks, paused, and turned to the stout, irritating man.

"Awa' an' bile yer heid!" she blared at him.

The crowd around her erupted and the man dissolved into the shadows.

Jock tried to pick them up at halftime in the Celtic dressing room. But it was a tough ask for him. They were down, on the ropes, bossed by the statuesque English legends.

"Come on, girls, you're better than this. We're better than this. We're showing them too much respect."

Amy's spirit rose to his words. Sensing the moment, and aware that it was slipping away, she burst forth.

"Come on, girls! If this is it, if this is the end, at least let's go down trying. Giving everything. I'm no' looking back on this thinking I could have done more. That's not happening!"

The whistle went for the second half. The Dick Kerr Ladies were already on the pitch, in their striped shirts and hats, knocking the ball around swiftly with slick ease. Amy looked at them with more determination than ever. Her buttons had been pressed. She meant business. The Fairfield Ladies team kicked off and Amy passed to Maggie McDougal, who immediately passed it back into midfield.

"What are you doin'?" Amy shouted. "We are nae goin' backwards! Forward! Forward!"

Fairfield Ladies were much better in the second half and some attacking play from their front five stopped the Dick Kerr Ladies from dominating possession in the way they had done in the first half. But, alas, it was still 2-0 to the English team.

In the 70th minute, one of the Fairfield defenders hit a long, loping ball over the last opposition defenders. Amy was onto it in a flash and pushed on, accelerating through the gears as she galloped ever nearer to the opposing goal.

As she cut through into the eighteen-yard box, she saw the tall, gangly goalkeeper start to come towards her, making herself look as big as she could with long, windmilling arms. Amy came a little nearer and then drew back her right boot, ready to unleash. The goalie took the bait and dived to her left. Amy then dropped her shoulders and darted to her right, skipping over the keeper's legs. She calmly passed the ball into the back of the net. Celtic Park erupted. Amy felt the roar course through her veins. She loved it.

Fairfield Ladies had more chances after this, and Amy very nearly got another, hitting the bar from a free kick. The game was now into its 90th minute and time was running out. In Amy's head, the irritating man, and his words, still echoed. She couldn't let him win. It couldn't happen.

She grabbed the ball from the sideline and cut infield. Her slender figure wove past a succession of Dick Kerr Ladies players. Why, she even nutmegged their indomitable captain, Alice Kell! She then swept the ball across the pitch to Sadie Moran and continued to run goalward.

Seconds later, Sadie pinged the ball back to Amy, who watched it in mid-air, as if it was in slow motion. She traced the ball as if it was a shooting star screeching across the sky. Then, like a ballerina, she rose into the air. Effortlessly timing her ascent to perfection, with her leg outstretched and perfectly horizontal, she met the ball with her white-laced boot. The perfect coming together. The keeper had no chance.

The whistle blew.

Chapter 42
The Library

Robbie's first training session with the girls went well, though it was a bit awkward at first. A group of teenage girls all standing uneasily in a vague huddle on the side of the pitch.

They were now without a manager. On the WhatsApp group they hadn't even mentioned Robbie. Why would they? They'd only get shot down by their mums and dads. Robbie Blair! The manager! Seriously! He's only fourteen himself! Sure, they would have all read about Robbie Blair. Sure, most would know he was destined to play for Celtic one day. Even the most cynical of cynics could see that. But the girls still didn't mention it. They knew, and that was what mattered. So they left it.

But he was here nonetheless, in his Celtic training kit and hoodie, RB on his back.

Robbie wasn't sure what to say. But he said it anyway.

"It's weird, isn't it? Me managing you. But I'm not your manager. I'm just a player like you. But I'll help you. I'll help you to achieve. I'm not going to tell you off. How sad would that be? I'm the same age as you! But I've seen you all play – I've been to most of your matches. I know how you play and I know how you think. If you want me to, I can help us progress as a team. I think we can still get something from the season. There are some games left. We can stay up. So, what do you think?"

The girls all nodded, sheepishly. Then Jamie stepped forth.

"Of course we want you, Robbie! You're what we need!" Jamie felt invigorated, the fire in her belly.

The girls echoed Jamie's words and cheered in approval.

"Yes, three cheers for Robbie Blair!" Isla chimed. Everyone laughed.

"Hip hip hooray, hip hip hooray, hip hip hooray!"

The girls threw their boaters in the air. The hats all careered like shooting stars and then fell down to earth like blossom on a summer's day. But Mallory Towers hadn't bizarrely transferred itself to Clydebank for one episode. It was still Clydebank and it had been a long time since they'd seen boats, never mind boaters!

But the girls were glad. They were glad Robbie was there. With them. Not at them. Not getting at them.

With them.

Training went well. After the girls had all been picked up, Jamie asked Robbie how he was getting back.

"Running, I guess."

"Well, my dad is struggling to pick me up. As it's only 2pm, do you fancy taking the train to Glasgow? There's something I need to find out. Something important."

"Yeah, no problem, I'm good with that."

Robbie Blair was always very amenable. Was he too amenable? Is there such a thing?

Maybe.

They took the train to Glasgow Central Station. Robbie felt a bit weird, sitting on the train in his mud-splattered kit. After a while, the mud on his thighs dried onto the acrylic check of the seat. He flexed his leg and flaked the mud off. Jamie noticed this and quickly whisked the mud up into her hands and took it to the nearest bin.

They stood by the train's automatic door. For Jamie, it took an eternity for the light to turn green. It always did. What if it never turned green? Would she be stuck there at the traffic management system, the pedestrian crossing, forever? What if it was never green?

But it was green. The door opened. Robbie got out.

Mind the gap!

Jamie looked at the all-encompassing divide that lay before her. The more she stared at it, the wider the gap became. And it was getting wider all the time.

Robbie looked at her. Imploringly. In a nice way.

"Come on, Jamie."

There was no exclamation mark, because he wasn't exclaiming anything. He was just asking her to 'come on'. Simples.

It was simple. It was really simple. To walk across, never mind jump, this great divide. What was so difficult?

Jamie would have prevaricated but there was a big queue behind her, bustling her. She felt it. She needed a big queue bustling behind her whenever she had an important decision to make. Was that possible?

They walked into the library. Jamie felt swamped by the sheer size of it all. She could see the stairs, but then she felt confused, because the staircase spiralled upwards, dissecting each floor. And each floor didn't seem separate to the last one, or the one before. They seemed to be one. Like a big gaping whale, taking in all the knowledge it could.

They struggled with the newfangled, transparent, multi-lingual lift and opted for the stairs instead.

"How many steps can there be?" Robbie asked.

There were a lot. Even for Robbie.

Eventually, they were there: the Archives Department. Robbie slumped down in a seat whilst Jamie approached the librarian.

"How can I help you today?" the lady asked. She had neat brown hair.

"I'm looking to find some information about a female Scottish footballer."

Without blinking, the lady asked for more details.

She looked at Jamie. Real close this time.

"What's she called?"

"Amy. Amy MacGregor. She was from Govan. She played in World War One for Fairfield Ladies."

"Just give me a minute," the librarian replied, in her best professional manner.

Jamie looked up and around, at the vaulted ceiling and then at Robbie. At Robbie's mud-splattered face. In a library.

Eventually, the librarian returned, clutching a handful of pages.

"This is what I've found. Newspaper articles and a copy of a family tree that includes your Amy MacGregor." The lady laid out the pages on the countertop in front of Jamie and continued:

"It appears that a lady called Gina used the genealogy department here to build a family tree a few years ago. She set the access to 'public' so that anyone could search and use it. Amateur family historians are quite helpful like that! Anyway, I have printed off the section that mentions your Amy."

Jamie looked at the family tree before her on the counter. Taking it all in, excitedly scribbling with a red pen, Jamie was ready to talk.

"OMG, Robbie! You are never going to believe this!"

"What?"

"The librarian only went and found that family tree that your Auntie Gina built when I first met you! You know, when you discovered that you were related to Fred."

Jamie paused for dramatic effect, the drum roll playing in her head whilst an increasingly confused Robbie looked at her.

"Amy MacGregor. She's Fred's mum! Your great-great uncle Fred. Our Fred."

"Aye," Robbie replied, taking it all in.

Amy MacGregor! Jamie thought. *The* Amy MacGregor. Her mum's Amy MacGregor. She was Fred's mum. Fred, who guided Robbie to where he is. Where he is now. *That* Fred.

Maybe he had guided her too, she thought.

It then hit her as she dozed on the train.

Maybe the old man helping her all those months ago at training ... maybe that had been Fred.

Gina's Family Tree

SERGAR CELTIC HISTORY

Chapter 43
The Pitch

Jamie lay in her bed and looked up at the ceiling. She felt exhausted, but also too alive to sleep. All those weeks and months of not being part of life. At all.

And now she was feeling fully alive.

Again.

Jamie hid in the trees. She felt small. Not scared, just nervous. Like a first day at school, maybe. Covering her eyes, but ready to look soon and be excited at the prospect. A hand had led her here.

Whose was it?

It wasn't Robbie's. Not this time. She could tell it was a soft, kind hand. She knew the hand. This familiar hand gently led Jamie through the trees and beyond.

Jamie. We're here.

Open your eyes, Jamie. What can you see?

What can you see?

Jamie opened her eyes and was blinded by the clarity of her sight. She squinted as she turned away. Falling away, her eyes looked down. Perfect grass, cut short and perfectly level. A beautiful lime green. Unbroken. She saw a white line painted onto the turf. She followed it around. A perfect circle. Her eyes were then drawn back to her feet. Her boots.

She couldn't remember putting them on.

Look, Jamie! Look!

Jamie looked to her right. The carpet of turf unravelled seamlessly towards the goal. And then again. Beyond it. A cascading, interlocking horizon of rooftops. All different, but all connected. And then, above them, the mountains. A Nordic green that gradually diluted to a misty grey. Staring down. From a distance. Jamie felt calm. Positive. Ready.

Then she looked left. It was blank. Nothing. She walked left. Drawn. She walked until the pitch ended. She looked down. A cliff. Rocks. Water. She felt sick. Her stomach began to swim, her heart raced and her mind swirled uncontrollably. She felt queasy as the waves roared over the jagged rocks below.

Was she here?

Or there?

Or both?

Then she heard the voice. Again.

It will never be perfect, Jamie.

But they are thoughts.

They are not you.

Chapter 44
The Save

It was Friday. The last day of Jamie's work experience.

Her dad had sorted out the work placement for her. She had thoroughly enjoyed the week. She had always had a natural affinity with kids. Her mum used to tell her that.

She hadn't been sure at first. And why would she? She hadn't been sure of anything. For ages. Nothing. She couldn't be sure she was capable of walking to the shop without swearing at someone, injuring someone, harming someone. She couldn't be certain of anything. What was real? What was not?

To Jamie, the children were children, not pupils. They were little kids, in hi-vis vests. They were happy and proud to be wearing those hi-vis vests. They were happy to be trotting along in a line. Along Dumbarton Road. Heading for the Town Hall Museum, to look at shipbuilding.

Mr McDougal led the line. Then there were five more children. Then Janet, a teaching assistant. Then another five children, and so on. Until you got to Jamie at the back of the line. Jamie wore a hi-vis vest too, and her thick, flaming locks contrasted with the vest.

All but one of the children had crossed the road. Just the one girl left. And then she stepped off the pavement. As if in slow motion. Soft Minecraft piano melodies rang out in the air. Everywhere. Elsie hadn't listened to Mr McDougal, who was no longer speaking. Everything that could help had stopped. Everything.

But not this.

Elsie walked into the middle of the road and then turned around. Why was she standing there?

The car loomed ever closer. Like a shark. It was poised to hit poor little Elsie.

But, suddenly, out of the blue...

See, Jamie had thought for years that 'out of the blue' was a pointless 'fronted adverbial phrase' that didn't mean anything.

But. Actually. Sometimes. It meant A LOT.

Out of the blue, Jamie ran into the road. She whisked Elsie into her arms. And saved her.

That's it.

Chapter 45
The Final

Today's the day.

Texts from Robbie pinged on Jamie's phone.

How do you feel? Last game. Against Stranraer. Win, and we stay up. This is our final!

Jamie felt sick. She stared into her cereal and stirred the milk around and around.

"Are you going to eat that, Jamie?" her dad asked, peering over his newspaper.

"Not sure."

Jamie barely felt like eating, even though she knew she had to. Amy MacGregor couldn't play football on an empty stomach, and neither could she. But she wasn't feeling it at all.

Her dad continued. "What time is your game, love?"

"The game? 1pm. Cathkin Park."

"Ok. I've got to pop to the uni, but I'll be there for 1pm. Are you looking forward to it?"

"No."

She stared into her cereal, almost hoping she could dive into the cool milk and swim away. From the pressure.

Robbie was going to meet her there. He had training in the morning. He'd posted a nice, upbeat message on the WhatsApp group, and the girls had all given him thumbs-ups.

Jamie took the train with Isla.

Isla tapped her under the table with her feet.

"Hey. You ok?"

Jamie didn't answer. Her mind was somewhere else.

"Hey! Jamie!"

"Uh, yeah?" she managed to reply, vaguely aware she was being spoken to.

"You ok, Jamie?"

Isla was a kind girl. She knew Jamie hadn't been well, and she often talked about her to her mum.

"I'm not feeling it, Isla. I dunnae know if I can play. I feel it's coming back. I've been feeling so good, too..."

"How?"

"I just feel dark again. As if someone's flicked a switch. Just like that."

"Cannae you just pretend it's not dark?"

"No. Not when it drags me in."

The girls made their way up the steps, through the curtain of trees, and then looked down onto the pitch. Jamie liked to come this way. It reminded her of when she came to Cathkin Park with Robbie and Hamish when they first met.

Robbie arrived with a friend of his from Celtic and put the girls through some basic shooting drills. He was still in his muddy shorts from his Celtic game.

Stranraer looked a slick-passing team. Robbie said they were decent and he'd seen them play a Celtic girls' team and they'd beaten them too.

Her dad just about made it on time. He gave Jamie a thumbs-up.

The first half was edgy. Clydebank just managed to keep it to 0-0, but there were a few nervy goal-line clearances. It was certainly a different experience for Robbie Blair. There was nothing he could do—no heroics for him to perform. He just had to stand and watch from the sideline with his teammate, Ruben, and somehow try to lift the girls from there.

The second half was similar. Robbie had got them working tightly as a team, looking out for each other, gelling as a unit. Jamie felt a little better than she had before the game, which wasn't saying a lot, but, in fairness, she hadn't had many opportunities come her way out on the left wing. But she still felt a little sick. She tried her best to block out all the noise and movement from the crowd and just concentrate on her game, as if she was back on the squash court. But it was difficult for her.

And then it happened.

Approaching the 88th minute, Jamie sensed an opportunity. She made a run and Isla played the perfect ball for her to dart onto. Jamie watched the ball in slow motion and timed her move to perfection. She felt Robbie urging her on.

Then it was just Jamie and the Stranraer keeper. She thought of Amy MacGregor. What would she do? What had Amy done in that final game? And then Jamie did it. She drew back her boot, ready to unleash her shot. Check. The keeper dived. Check.

But then, just as Jamie went to skip over the keeper's outstretched legs, the desperate goalie clipped Jamie's boots and she went tumbling over into the wet grass.

Penalty!

Now, when Jamie had been away, Elspeth had taken the penalties. Elspeth grabbed the ball and held it close to her.

"Give it to Jamie!" came the voice. It was Robbie, loud and clear from the sideline.

Jamie looked at Robbie. She looked scared. He looked at her. Though he was half the pitch away, it was as if he was right next to her.

"Take it," he said.

Elspeth gave the ball to Jamie. She started her slow walk to the penalty spot.

Jamie placed the ball. She stepped back. What would she do? Pick her spot and go for it or wait? React in the moment?

She approached the ball. And then, at the last moment. In the very last moment. She saw. She saw the keeper start to dive to her left.

She did know things.

She did know what she had done and what she had not done. Seen and not seen. She really was in charge of her own mind. She saw this now, and she saw it at this crucial moment.

She was a good person. And she tried her best. She was enough.

Always.

The End

JG Nolan

Dear Diary

Hello! I'm older now. But I'm still Jamie. I'm still the girl who's writing these words.

Still the girl in this book.

I've been thinking. You know, if you're like me and think like me, poor you. I feel sorry for you. You're doomed. Ha! No, I don't really think that, and I KNOW that you know I don't think that. Don't you? I literally just slapped myself in the face ☹

The thing is... Ha! Thing! What is a thing? Really? Shouldn't it be just like a sandwich filling? Just that. Shut up. Enough.

This has been difficult for me, you know, this whole journey. But I also know that it's never going to end. The way I think about things is difficult. I am difficult. Like I say, it's a journey, but I feel I am getting there. Even though it doesn't feel like it sometimes...

I will never stop the way I think. The thoughts. But I am me, and I can choose how I respond to them. The thoughts.

I can never know anything for certain.

Who does?

But deep down, I know I'm ok.

I'm an ok person and I try my best.

Well, at the end of the day, as Robbie would say, you always need something to look forward to.

So, keep looking forward.

I'll see you soon.

Jamie

A note from JG Nolan
Squash

I think playing sport and keeping fit is really, really important for every-one – of all ages.

That's why sport is always in my books. I have always loved football and always will do but you will notice, if you have got to the end of this book, that I make lots of mentions of squash! I have played squash since I was 5 and I am 51 now! Wait! – I should be way better than I am ...

Ah well, moving on, Jump2 features a rather lovely squash club called Brookside and this squash club does actually exist. I took the inspiration from Brookside Squash Club in Bronygarth, Wales. I have played there for many years and have often wandered down the narrow tree-lined lane in search of my next squash assignment, whilst the babbling brook flows beneath me. I also want to mention my own squash club, Shrewsbury Squash and Racket Ball Club. Sitting on the outskirts of Shrewsbury, under the shadow of Haughmond Hill, the club has been a massive in-fluence on me and, in a way, is my second home. In fact, my whole family can be found there most days! Three generations of Nolans have spent most of their waking hours on the courts there! I have played there my entire life and now coach juniors and adults and captain teams. Squash is a great sport because it involves speed, fitness and mental strength – hopefully, you see all of these attributes in all of the Jump! books.

JG Nolan's
Squash
Inspiration for JUMP2

Brookside Squash and Racketball Club

INSPIRATION

Shropshire squash sensation named volunteer of the year

2024

AKA legend!

Dad/Papa/Cyril

Alex

My boys!

Alex & Robbie

'Our' Robbie

Alex, JG & Dad

Visit the Sergar Creative website and hit the subscribe button to be the first to hear news about JUMP!

Former England, Celtic and Manchester City Goalkeeper Joe Hart contributed the foreword for JUMP!

The following quotes have been taken from reviews submitted by readers to various internet platforms.

"A story of overcoming adversity, of dreams, of fantasy, of connecting with the past, and mysterious influences; some great drawings in there too! Is it a children's book? Well, I'm 70..."

"This is a moving and uplifting story. I enjoyed reading from start to finish."

"A heartwarming story about overcoming challenges - as a sports person, I really related to this and highly recommend it to anyone!"

"This is a great read! Robbie Blair is awesome with his never-say-die attitude. I can imagine people of all ages getting something from Jump!"

"As a runner who has setbacks through injury in the past, I can resonate with Robbie that determination and perseverance triumphs. A fantastic read for all the family."

"A 'must-read' for anyone of any age seeking inspiration"

"The story of Robbie Blair, who overcomes the odds time and time again to become a success on the football field, is a heartwarming read for children and adults. Its messages of hope and perseverance, woven into a captivating story which brings past and present together in a very readable story kept me turning the pages and not wanting to put it down. It has ageless appeal."

"Excellent. Uplifting. Emotional rollercoaster of a read"

"Robbie's determination makes you believe that anything is possible. This book is an amazing read and I would definitely recommend."

"Jump is a joyous read. It's about following your dreams, overcoming setbacks and hard work. Jump made me laugh, it made me sad and it made me nervous! I believed in the characters, the story and its messages, really never a dull passage or a wasted line. Wonderfully written and beautifully illustrated, it's a book suitable for all kids and adults; being a footy fan is not required."

"This could be Generation Z's Billy Elliot!"

Classroom activities around Jump 2 would work best with Years 8 and 9
(ages 12 to 14)

Triggers:- bereavement, mental health – specifically OCD

---◆◯◆---

Ongoing Reading Journal Activities

Dear Diary entries

Use these sections to track Jamie's emotions, mood and feelings
throughout the story.

□ Why has the author used italics for some parts of Jamie's diary
entries?

□ The author uses italics throughout the book. What is the purpose
and significance of these?

□ Please take note of all the factors that help Jamie on her journey.
How and why are these things significant?

Mountain chapters

□ Why has the author included these four chapters?

□ Can you summarise what these chapters mean?

Activities based on chapters while reading

<u>Chapters 1–4</u>

□ What does the author mean by the sentence 'The blue skies became grey, and Jamie thought she would never hear the birds sing again.'?

□ Jamie doesn't want to move house. What evidence can you find to support this statement?

□ In this chapter, Jamie meets her new football coach, Bruce. How do you feel towards both characters after reading this chapter?

<u>Chapters 5–7</u>

□ What is making Jamie's dad constantly late for work?

□ 'It would be good if she could carry Robbie around everywhere she went.' – What does Jamie mean by this?

□ How do Jamie and Robbie differ in their reaction to the cooker possibly being left on?

<u>Chapters 8–12</u>

□ What does the repeated use of 'again' tell us about Jamie's mood?

□ In chapter 8, we hear of Amy for the first time. How might she and Robbie help Jamie?

□ 'She knew she had to continue.' What does the author mean by this?

□ What is the role of the therapist?

□ Compare and contrast this therapist with the therapist Jamie met in chapter 6.

□ Explore Jamie's feelings. How and why do her feelings change? What adjectives could describe her feelings?

□ Summarise this chapter in one sentence.

Chapter 13

☐ Why might chapter 13 be taking place two weeks after the previous chapter?

☐ Why doesn't Jamie want to sleep again?

Chapters 14–17

☐ 'And that was a start'. What is the significance of 'The Great Bukovski'?

☐ Jamie always takes Robbie's advice. Why do you think this might be?

☐ We are introduced to the painter in chapter 17. Follow this character through the remainder of the story. Where does he appear? Why might the author have introduced him? What is the painter's role in the story?

Chapter 18

☐ Compare and contrast what we learn about Amy with what we know about Jamie.

Chapters 19–22

☐ In Jamie's mind, what might be the message behind the painter's words at the end of chapter 19? Why are the words in her mind?

☐ Describe in your own words why Robbie has arrived at Jamie's aunt's house.

Chapters 23–28

☐ Can you see a link between Amy and Jamie in these chapters? What is it?

☐ Amy says she can see a reason for her being at Craiglockhart Hospital. Why might the author have included Amy in the story?

□ Amy ensures she speaks to Jack during the day 'when he was still there.' – What does this mean? Where does he go at night? What evidence can you find to support your ideas?

Chapters 30–32

□ How do Jamie's and Robbie's experiences in these chapters mirror those of Amy's and Jack's?

□ Robbie can see a change in Jamie. What is this change? How might discovering the squash court have contributed to this?

□ Why does Jamie say "Thanks, Mum!" when she decides to play squash?

□ Why has the author included the older man at the squash court?

Chapters 33–35

□ Why do you think Jamie is dreaming about the battle in chapter 33?

□ What language has the author used to show the horrors of war?

□ Water features heavily in chapter 34 as a metaphor for Jamie's recovery. Do you agree with this statement? Give examples.

□ What do you think Jamie has learned by attending the music club? Why would this be good for her?

Chapter 36

□ Auntie Jackie says, "Hopefully, it's been good for you." What would your response be?

□ The painter reminds Jamie that we forget 'moments of sunshine'. – What does he mean by this?

Chapters 37–40

☐ Describe and explain how and why Robbie helps Jamie in these chapters.

☐ In what ways are Jamie and Robbie similar and different?

☐ Jamie runs throughout the story. Explain how running is important to Jamie on her route to recovery.

☐ Why do you think memories are essential in Jump 2?

Chapter 41

☐ Why do you think this was Amy's last football game?

Chapter 42

☐ At the library, Robbie and Jamie discover Amy's identity. How might this explain the connection between Amy and Jamie?

Chapters 43–45

☐ Jamie demonstrates increased confidence and positivity. How?

☐ What do you think she has learned about herself?

☐ Overall, in what ways has Jamie become better during the book and how has this been achieved?

☐ Why do we not find out whether the penalty is successful?

☐ How does this contrast with the final chapter of Jump!?

☐ The subheading for Jump 2 is 'You are enough.' – What do you think this means?

☐ Write a book review or fill in a response grid detailing likes, dislikes, questions and links.

<u>Further activities</u>

☐ Research women's football during WW1 and the early part of the twentieth century.

For additional classroom material or to submit a question to JG Nolan Please scan this QR code

Or email info@sergarcreative.co.uk with questions, requests for video responses or to enquire about author visits to your school.

BV - #0010 - 150824 - C18 - 216/138/11 - PB - 9781739208424 - Matt Lamination